EXCELLER SELECT

TOP PICKS

THE LAUGHTER RIOT

THE LAUGHTER RIOT

The Adventures of Goldie and Other Stories

PRIYAMITA GHOSH

EXCELLER BOOKS®
A GLOBAL PRESS

The Laughter Riot
The Adventures of Goldie and Other Stories

Cover design by Tama Mondal
Cover and interior Illustrations by Priyasri Ghosh

ISBN: 978-93-47397-53-0

Published in India in 2025 by Exceller Books,
An imprint of GE Group
G1, Dream Apartment, Degree College Road, Belgharia,
Kolkata, 700056, India
www.excellerbooks.com

EXCELLER BOOKS®
A GLOBAL PRESS

Dedication

Dedicated to my darling daughter.
May her life be filled with joy and laughter.

Acknowledgement

To be honest, I never thought that I would actually write a book. I have a full-time job and a little daughter (so that makes it two full-time jobs!).

I first wrote a few stories when I was a prisoner at home during the COVID lockdown. While my friends indulged in a plethora of activities, such as cooking, singing, and painting, I decided that I would write a few funny one-liners. These one-liners evolved into dialogue and imaginary fictional characters, soon unfolding into short stories. I initially penned down a few real-life anecdotes on social media (like my wedding, my viva exam in college, etc.) These were widely appreciated in a few social media groups, which led me to create a few fictional characters like Mishti Mashi and Goldie. To my surprise, my readers related to these characters deeply and encouraged me to write more. For this, I am sincerely indebted to my first few readers. Their heartfelt appreciation gave me the confidence to pen down more stories. After a year or so, I seriously considered compiling these stories and publishing a book.

I would like to thank my family for their unwavering support and appreciation while I wrote these stories; my husband for his honest remarks about several of the stories I wrote; and my little daughter, who keeps babbling to anyone who will listen, proudly proclaiming that her mother is an author. I would also like to thank my publisher for giving me this opportunity and for having faith in a budding writer.

Although all these stories and characters are fictional, I have studied the nuances and quirks (or idiosyncrasies, if you will) of several friends and family members, and these quirks in their personalities have been depicted in my stories.

Many of my readers have requested that they want to meet my Mishti Mashi and my cousin Goldie, but alas, these are all fictional characters — a figment of my overactive imagination! Having said that, I must also add that a few anecdotes pertain to my real life as well, viz., the story about the viva and the story of my wedding, and so on. I really hope that this book of funny stories is 'just what the doctor ordered'!

Table of Contents

The Adventures of My Cousin Goldie

Goldie and the Red Notebook

It was the beginning of my winter vacation, and I was spending a week at my cousin Goldie's house. You remember my cousin Goldie? His mother had named him Goldie because she thought he had a heart of gold. I do not know about the 'heart of gold' bit, but he had a gold tooth that glinted whenever he opened his mouth, like a goldfish.

I was 15 years old and Goldie was 13. He was not young and stupid anymore — he was old and stupid. If you want to know more about Goldie, I can tell you that he was somewhat rectangular in shape, and one must not assume that he had a good personality just because he was not good-looking. His superpower was making people laugh, which would have been wonderful if he had tried to make them laugh, but he was the butt of jokes himself. He was always complaining about me that I never listened to him… or something like that.

Now, I do not know whether any of my readers know it, and I certainly do not want to brag, but I am a decent artist. Yes, in fact, I spent the long winter afternoons sketching funny caricatures of my family members. Goldie's father (my uncle) formed the central character of my sketches.

I had a red-covered drawing book in which I had doodled several such sketches. The first page captured my uncle stuffing his face with sandwiches with one hand while grabbing a chicken leg with the other, asking, "What's for dessert?" as my aunt scowled at him. The second page showed him salivating, while looking longingly at a goat, and I had written: "Mutton rhymes with glutton."

In the third page, he was thrusting fistfuls of cashews into his mouth, and I had captioned it: "You are what you eat, so lay off the nuts." The next page contained the masterpiece — a lady was asking him, "I love what you have done with your hair, how you get it to come out of your nostrils like that?" I am not boasting, but that book was like a car accident; if you looked at it once, you couldn't look away.

However, this uncle of mine was a lawyer and quite an intimidating specimen. I am not saying that all lawyers are bad; it's just that 99% of them give the other 1% a bad name. He was gigantic — about 7 feet tall and almost 5 feet in width, I suppose. As kids, we seldom went to my uncle's room and stayed out of his way. Let's just say, some uncles are lovable and full of sweet charm, and others are not quite so full. He belonged to the latter club. To add to the list, he was also arrogant. He acted as if he knew everything. The people who always act like they know everything are really irritating for those of us who do. All relatives are bad enough, but uncles are the worst. I think uncles, as a race, are solely responsible for our unhealthy coping mechanisms in childhood and contribute greatly to the development of sarcasm and a dark sense of humour, later in our lives.

So, it was a Sunday, and my winter vacation stretched ahead of me. We all just had a sumptuous lunch. My aunt was a marvellous cook who had the divine fire in her. That day, she had really outdone herself. From a Michelin-star-worthy *shukto*, we proceeded to some toothsome fish-cutlets and from these toothsome fish-cutlets, we went slowly but surely to some Mutton curry that even Sanjeev would have been proud to sponsor (not Sanjeev Kumar, the actor, silly... Sanjeev Kapoor, the chef). From thereon, our palate was slathered by some tangy pineapple chutney, and finally, the *gurer payesh* passed over the epiglottis with a good deal of vim, locking in the sweet memory. In a nutshell, it was a great Sunday. In fact, it was the Sundayest Sunday that had ever Sundayed in a while.

Now, my uncle was recently diagnosed with Diabetes, so my aunt kept him under the strictest vigil. He had a sweet tooth but was not allowed to even touch the chutney or *payesh* in her presence, yet he looked longingly while we golfed, heaping spoonfuls of the delicacies into our systems. After lunch, he sat dismally in front of the TV while we retired to the veranda.

The sky was bright and sunny, and we were blessed with lovely weather. My school seemed miles away (which it was, of course), and the day stretched endlessly ahead. A blissful void of the mind and a soothing, peaceful cloud seemed to permeate into the soul.

Suddenly, with a jolt, I remembered I had left the red sketch-book on the dining table. It was with me while I had lunch, and then I went to wash my hands, and one couldn't help but wonder what the upshot would be if the said book were to fall into the wrong hands.

I bolted downstairs to the dining hall, but to my dismay, I saw the book was not there. I immediately went and asked Shibu where it was. Shibu was a 17-year-old boy whose mother was the domestic help, and he spent his time running errands for my uncle.

"Shibu, *amar laal kata ta dekhechhish*?" I asked urgently, peeking into the kitchen.

"Hya," Shibu replied casually, wiping his hands. *"Tomar kaku toh ota ghore niye geche."*

My eyes widened. *"Ki? Kokhon?"*

To my utter dismay, he told us that Uncle had picked up the notebook after lunch, noted its contents, and grimly taken it to his room, where he kept it on top of the almirah. He found it strange that he should keep a book on top of the almirah and looked at us questioningly.

I told Goldie to go and fetch the book immediately.

The conversation was as follows:

Me: "Goldie, you have to save me. Run along and get the book before Uncle comes to his room."

Goldie: "What! I can't go now. Why are you in such a hurry?

Let's just take it slow and think of another plan."

Me: "You know what happens to folks who are slow and steady, *na*?"

Goldie: "They win the race?"

Me: "No, they get killed in the fire. Now, you are the organized one. You are always neatly arranging stuff. If he catches you, say you were cleaning his room."

Goldie: "That's true, I am very organized. I love a clean room and a clean desk. Do you know that a clean desk is a sign of…?"

Me: "A cluttered drawer?"

Goldie: "No. Why can't you clean your room? You are unmotivated, lazy."

Me: "Not at all. It's just that I am highly motivated to stay put
in one place and do nothing. *Acha*, Goldie, you are just like Bruce Lee, your hero. You can do this. Just go to his room, *na*."

Goldie: "Yes, I do have a lot in common with Bruce…"

Me: "Of course you do. If you just take away the looks, money, charm and success, there's hardly any difference between you and him."

Goldie: "Physical appearance and material possessions can never stand in my way."

Me: "What about your crappy personality?"

Goldie: "Why are you hell-bent on being sarcastic and destroying my happiness?"

Me: "Because I derive a lot of happiness from it. Just shut your mouth when you are talking to me, *na*."

Goldie was getting on my nerves. He was slower than a herd of turtles stampeding over butter. I had no choice but to implore Shibu to get the notebook. Shibu, sensing some lurking peril, gravely declined to go to Uncle's room. We even offered him Rs. 50 to go and get it. He just stood there and shook his head obstinately. After much coaxing, he proved to be an honest fellow and faithful friend and decided to help us (when we had doubled the bribe, of course).

We crouched behind the sofa while Shibu went on the expedition to recover the notebook. Uncle was still watching TV downstairs, so we thought it would be safe for Shibu to go right away.

However, just as Shibu stepped on a chair to retrieve the notebook, Uncle came upstairs and caught him red-handed. I looked at him from our hiding place, and I must say that he looked menacing. I have seen untwinkling eyes before, but never a pair so free of twinkle as his.

Shibu was mumbling something incoherent and was standing against the wall and trying, it seemed, to move through it like Harry Potter. Failing in the endeavour, he simply stood there trembling like a blanc-mange and making a gurgling sound.

Uncle looked more intimidating than ever. He seemed to have grown a bit after lunch; no doubt the burgeoning of his constitution could be attributed to the kilos of mutton he had consumed. He was at least 8 feet 2 now and about 6 feet in width.

To our horror, he came out of the room and locked the door from the outside. Muttering under his breath, he went downstairs again to watch TV.

"What do we do now, Goldie?" I asked, pacing nervously.

"We can run away," he suggested, eyes already darting toward the door.

"And leave Shibu locked inside? Absolutely not." I jabbed a finger at him. "You unlock the door and free him."

Goldie gulped. "But what if Dad comes?"

I sighed theatrically. "You disappoint me, Goldie. I thought you had guts."

"I do!" he protested weakly. "I just don't want them twisted by his bare hands."

"Don't underestimate your abilities—*that's* my job," I smirked. "You know what, you remind me of a coin."

He perked up slightly. "You mean I'm valuable?"

"No," I said sweetly. "You're worthless and double-faced."

Goldie slumped again. "I just wish I knew magic."

"Yes," I replied, rolling my eyes. "I also wish you'd do a disappearing act right now."

He glared at me. "I thought you were brave."

"My bravery," I said, placing a hand dramatically on my chest, "is like my underwear—I do have it, but I don't necessarily want to show it off."

Goldie groaned. "Oh dear, Dad will hate me now. I'm his only child. I always thought I was the reason he smiled every day."

"I thought," I said with a wicked grin, "you were the reason he drinks."

Goldie closed his eyes, deep in thought. I liked seeing him with his eyes closed, and I liked seeing him even more with my eyes closed.

Well, I had no choice but to free Shibu. I tip-toed to the room and unlocked the door. At first, there were no signs of Shibu, but then I located him under the bed. His face was pale. He crawled out on all fours, and we left the room.

After restoring democracy once again, the three of us had a conference.

Shibu's voice trembled as he whispered, *"Babu jodi police ke daake?"*

I stared at him, confused. *"Keno? Tui kichu churi korechis naki? Eto bhoy pacchis keno?"*

My readers may have noticed that Goldie was not participating in the dialogue, and that was because he had inhaled a mosquito and was choking silently against the background. I was too engrossed in thought to bother about choking cousins.

I went into my uncle's room once again to look around and formulate a plan. You may all know by now that I have a subtle and scheming intellect — I think quickly and I act quickly. Hitler was also known to do the same, and so, for that matter, was Akbar the Great. I looked around the room and started browsing through his books (mostly on law).

Uncle came to his room after around two hours. He looked at me menacingly and muttered, "Who unlocked this door?"

"Yes, I did," I admitted.

Uncle's tone turned sharp, the earlier warmth gone. "May I know why?"

"I didn't want you to fall into trouble," I replied, trying to sound sensible and noble.

"*Me*? In trouble?" he let out a cold chuckle. "No, no, it's *you*, young lady—though I'm not entirely sure I should even call you a 'lady'—who is in very deep waters."

I folded my arms, refusing to be intimidated. "Oh, I don't think so."

His face changed colour and became a bright shade of magenta. A vein had popped out of nowhere in his forehead. Anyone in my position would have wilted under his gaze.

Uncle narrowed his eyes. "Would you care to elaborate?"

"Oh, certainly!" I replied, clearing my throat with dramatic importance. "You see, you locked Shibu in that room. If I'm not mistaken, that act falls under Sections 359 to 369 of the IPC—specifically relating to kidnapping or child stealing, which essentially means taking away a girl below sixteen or a boy below eighteen from the lawful custody of his or her parent..."

"WHAT?" Uncle exploded. "I didn't take him away! He was in *my* room!"

"Ah, yes," I nodded sympathetically, "but he was locked inside *against his will* for two whole hours. And if he knew better, he'd press charges. Do you know his uncle works as a chauffeur for another law firm? If Shibu decides to confide in him, that lawyer would *jump* at the opportunity..."

I noticed a flicker of fear in his eyes.

"Kidnapping is just like college, Uncle—only in reverse," I said matter-of-factly.

He stared at me, bewildered. "What? How?"

"Well," I explained with a shrug, "colleges demand a huge amount of money to keep your child *away* and if you don't pay, they threaten to send them back home."

I could see that my wisecrack was ill-timed. His face had now turned a rich shade of purple.

Uncle massaged his temples. "Wait, wait, surely Shibu didn't say he would do anything like that."

"Of course not," I said proudly. "Not *after* I bribed him with a whole stash of chocolates from under your bed! Speaking of which, why are you hiding chocolates under your bed even after being diagnosed with diabetes? I'm fairly certain Auntie would not approve."

Uncle froze, eyes widening. "Never mind about the chocolates." His voice dropped to a sharp whisper. "Did he take something from my room? A notebook, perhaps?"

I could see his eyes gleaming vindictively. I merely folded my arms and gave him a longish stare in which hauteur and contempt were mixed in equal proportion.

"Oh yes," I said quickly, nodding. "It was my sketch-book. He thought I must have misplaced it."

"I see," Uncle's gaze sharpened. "May I say a thing or two about that sketch-book of yours?"

I noticed the offensive smugness in his countenance, a characteristic of uncles in general and my uncle in particular.

"Not unless you want Auntie to know about the hidden stash of chocolates," I replied sweetly.

Blackmail is a wonderful thing—unless, of course, you're on the receiving end of it.

Uncle's jaw tightened. "I see."

"Well, you should look at the *bright* side of reading that book," I suggested, trying to sound encouraging.

"I couldn't find any bright side," he grumbled.

"Oh, but you did," I said with a triumphant grin. "You discovered that your eyesight is still absolutely perfect."

He exhaled, defeated. "You are a pesky kid, but I'm not judging you."

I wanted to tell him that I, too, didn't judge him even though he drank mutton gravy like a beverage, but I maintained a dignified silence.

He, in turn, made a sound like a cat swallowing a watermelon but refrained from further dialogue.

"Well, that's that," I said, dusting off my hands as if concluding a business deal. "Now, I shall take your leave. I've removed all traces of evidence—namely, the chocolates. I couldn't leave them there, you understand. Shibu might tell Auntie. He *really* cares about your health."

Uncle looked as if he were silently calculating all his mistakes.

"Anyway," I continued cheerfully, "he won't press charges. I told him you were kind enough to give him all the chocolates *and* a hundred-rupee note."

When uncle spoke, his voice was like that of a new mother cooing to her baby — I would not have thought it possible that such cooing could have come from his larynx.

"Oh, come, come, no need to bribe him," Uncle said, attempting a reassuring smile. "Shibu is a good boy. He won't do anything foolish."

I couldn't help myself—I let out a low, sardonic laugh.

"A small price to pay," I said sweetly, "for not being labelled a kidnapper, don't you think?"

An indubitably unpleasant grunt escaped from his lips. He could not have been glaring at me with more obvious distaste if I were the fly in his mutton.

I could not resist shooting a quick glance towards Goldie (who had listened to the entire conversation from his hiding-place) and felt satisfied to note the worshipping awe in his countenance.

Uncle was also impressed, but not as favourably as Goldie. He was struggling for utterance. For a moment, he just stood there wordlessly, and then he said, "Okay".

Then his moustache parted in what can only be termed a conciliatory smile. After that, he coughed up the hundred-rupee note and retired to his room.

I also returned to my room and feasted on a well-deserved chocolate or two.

Durga Puja with Goldie

Most of you who have read my stories will be well-acquainted with my cousin Goldie. He was nicknamed Goldie by his mother (my aunt), who thought he was as valuable as solid gold, whereas I always thought he was more of a goldfish material. I mean, let's put it this way, if he ever underwent an IQ test, he would definitely test negative! I suppose he had just about enough intelligence to eat and sleep by himself, but certainly not much more. Anyway, my mother always said that he was not all that bad. 'He grows on people', but then, so does cancer, right?

He did not have too many enemies, but was immensely unpopular in our family. He was somewhat rectangular in shape, meaning that though Mother Nature had ensured his growth with time, he had merely been stretched sideways and not much in height. Hence, he would be best described as egg-shaped or rectangular.

I was around 13 then, and Goldie was 15. I had gone to spend my Puja vacation at his place.

The story unfolds like this.

My aunt (Goldie's mum) called me one fine morning.

"Hey, what are you doing this *pujo*?"

Durga Puja was around the corner, and my aunt always invited me to stay over at their place. My aunt was not as bad as some of my other relatives; she was definitely worse. I always found an excuse to avoid her.

Before I could respond, she gushed, "Isn't it lovely having such a big family — cousins, aunts, uncles...I always say that happiness comes from having a big, caring family."

I hesitated before speaking. "In another country, right?" I asked quietly.

Aunt looked puzzled. "What?"

"Nothing." I murmured, trying to avoid her gaze. "I may not be able to go this year."

She immediately shook her head, her voice firm and warm at the same time. "No, no, you must come."

I knew I was defeated. There are two ways to argue with an aunt, but neither worked. It is often said that hell hath no fury like an aunt turned down or something like that, and so, grudgingly, I surrendered.

Aunt's eyes suddenly lit up. "Hey, I have an idea. Do you know what you should do?"

I raised an eyebrow, pretending to be very serious. "No, please, enlighten me—while I take notes."

She chuckled softly, leaning closer as if about to share a big secret. "Let me give you some advice."

As a rule, I always advise people never to give me any advice, but no one takes my advice.

Aunt folded her arms and gave me a mock stern look. "I told you on WhatsApp too. Let's wear matching colours on each day of the *pujo* and click lots of photos." Then she leaned forward, her expression turning suspicious. "*Achha,* tell me—

why haven't you replied to my WhatsApp messages? I've sent you so many inspirational forwards."

Her inspirational WhatsApp messages every morning had inspired me to block her about a month ago.

I shrugged innocently and said, "Oh, I think I may have misplaced your number."

When I said I lost her number, I meant it was lost after I hit the 'delete' button.

Aunt's voice softened, almost pleading. "Please, let's celebrate this *pujo* the way I'm suggesting."

I didn't want to promise anything yet, so I offered a noncommittal smile. "I'll think about it."

When I said "I'll think about it," what I really meant was that I would forget about it until she brought it up again.

So, to cut a long story short, I was at Goldie's place during the *pujo*. However, Goldie had a bad cold on the first day of *pujo* and his mother had forbidden him to go pandal-hopping with us. By 'us', I mean a group of five friends, including Aditi, Goldie's neighbour. Now, Goldie had a crush on Aditi and was heartbroken that he could not go pandal-hopping with us.

After three days, Goldie was almost in tears! He badly wanted to go out but did not have the guts to disobey his mother. He looked at me imploringly, and I promised to help him because of the kindness in my heart and, more importantly, the fact that he had promised to buy me an extra pair of shoes with his pocket money!

I leaned towards Goldie, lowering my voice like a secret agent planning an escape. "Let's chalk out a plan, Goldie. How can we get you out of this house? Hmm, let's think."

Goldie, ever the dramatic one, flipped open a notebook. "Let's write down all the clever thoughts in our heads in paragraphs."

I could not resist teasing him. "Oh, come on. If you write down all the clever thoughts in *your* head, you'll win a prize for the shortest paragraph ever."

He did not get my joke. Instead, always a glutton for punishment, he stared at himself in the mirror.

He slumped back dramatically, frustration written all over his face. "My parents don't let me do anything. *Uff,* I just hate my life."

I let out a dry laugh. "You hate your life, do you? Come, join the club—it's called *Everybody.*"

I racked my brains for a devious plan that would ensure that Goldie could leave the house unnoticed. Intense thinking had rendered me rather hungry, so I raided the fridge, and that's when I found it — a can of tuna! I nicked it deftly and tip-toed to my room before anybody could notice. I filled Goldie in on my plot.

That night, around 2am, when everyone was immersed in deep slumber after the *pujo* festivities, Goldie and I sneaked into the kitchen and put spoonfuls of tuna into the cups and glasses on the top-most shelves.

By the next afternoon, the kitchen reeked of raw fish and the entire household was in complete disarray — nobody could locate the source of this ghastly odour! My aunt looked hassled, "Did anyone see a cat? I'm sure the cat ate some fish here in the kitchen this morning."

The drowsy stillness of the afternoon was shattered by the cacophony of a gaggle of aunts hunting for a cat! When the search for the fiend in feline form in the kitchen proved futile, the posse moved positions and started moving the furniture around, checking under the sofa and beds.

While this mayhem ensued, I had sneaked Goldie out of his room, and we went out with our friends.

Feeling more courageous than ever, I proposed that we all go to the nearest theatre for a movie.

Goldie initially agreed, but after a few minutes, protested, "No, no, I have changed my mind."

"So, does this one work any better?" I asked, gesturing toward the plan laid out before us.

Goldie's eyes widened in panic. "What? No! If I'm late, my parents will definitely scold me."

I crossed my arms and gave him a challenging look. "Do you really want to look like a spineless cowardly-custard in front of Aditi?"

Goldie opened and shut his mouth like a goldfish. If he had a mind, I figured that there was something on it.

Goldie puffed out his chest slightly. "No, of course not."

I gave him a look of exaggerated relief. "Seriously, Goldie, thank God stupidity isn't a crime, or you'd have been arrested long ago."

He groaned, throwing his hands in the air. "*Uff*, why do you want to annoy me right now?"

"Trust me," I said innocently, "annoying you is the *last* thing I want to do." I paused, and then added with a smirk, "However, it's still on the list."

Goldie frowned, trying to maintain his dignity. "Strong people don't put others down."

"Of course not," I replied, nodding sagely. "They lift them up and then throw them face-first on the floor—for maximum damage." His expression only grew gloomier, so I nudged him lightly. "Come on, don't look so upset. Look at me—I can laugh at myself, and in case you can't, I'd be happy to do it for you too."

He squinted at me. "Oh, you think you're the only one with a sense of humour?"

"Of course not," I shot back instantly. "You're living proof that God also has a sense of humour."

Goldie glared. "Shut up, don't talk like an idiot."

"But then," I asked sweetly, "how else would you understand me?"

He folded his arms dramatically. "Let me think. I am lost in thoughts right now."

"Well, of course you're lost," I said with a grin. "It must be unfamiliar territory for you."

After our endless banter, he mustered up some courage and agreed to go for a movie! Goldie looked happy. In fact, he was overjoyed to be able to go out with Aditi. His face was glowing so much that it was difficult, at that moment, to distinguish him from a ray of sunshine.

He even shared his popcorn with Aditi, and that is saying something, because he NEVER shared anything ever! In fact, the only thing he had shared willingly with me, since childhood, was chickenpox!

After the movie, we came home surreptitiously and just as Goldie was tip-toeing to his room, his father spotted him.

"Goldie! Come here."

Now, this uncle (Goldie's father) of mine was a grim, bespectacled and snarky one — always testy. The word which best described him would be 'waspish', I suppose. He was definitely not the type of uncle whose eyes you covered with your hands over the breakfast table and cooed, "Guess who!"

We usually maintained a 3-metre radius around him at any given time.

Goldie hissed into my ear, "Now, do you regret lying?"

I sighed dramatically. "No, I don't regret doing any of this. I regret getting caught. And just so you know—I'm blaming you if anything goes wrong."

Goldie looked offended. "Come on, it wasn't my fault."

"I never said it was your fault," I replied with a sly grin. "I just said I'm going to blame you."

Both of us walked up slowly to him. Goldie stood there, averting his gaze and looking at his toes or thereabouts.

"Well, uncle, how was your day?" I chirruped, endeavouring to clear the air, which was smelling of tuna and deceit.

Uncle said, "Hmm, I am given to understand that Goldie was supposed to be in his room all day, owing to his flu."

I looked at Goldie. His face ranged in colour from coral to salmon. It was fun to watch, but I came to his rescue!

"I took Goldie out to pray at the nearby pandal," I explained, trying to sound as saintly as possible. "I wanted Ma Durga to help him recover quickly."

Uncle raised an eyebrow, unimpressed. "It took you three hours to pray?"

His steely gaze darted between our faces, and I noticed that Goldie's face had turned magenta!

It would not be entirely out of context here to mention that the allure of questioning, grilling, or even hunting lay in whether one is at the right or wrong end of the gun. Uncle's implacable gaze cut through us like a knife, and I believe, in that moment, if he were cast to play the role of Shylock, he could have done it without a rehearsal.

Without batting an eyelid or pausing for breath, I replied with the smoothness of cold cream, "Well, after praying, we walked to another pandal and then Goldie's legs were aching, so we took a cab to return home. However, on our way back, the cab had a tyre-puncture and so we waited, while the cabbie fixed the tyre."

I looked triumphantly while Goldie let out his breath slowly. However, I could see that my ebullient nature and confident reply cut no ice with my uncle.

Uncle looked at Goldie with a mix of surprise and amusement. "I had no idea he was so devoted to praying. Clearly, he has qualities I've never seen before."

I suppose this was the moment for rattling off all the good qualities of Goldie, one by one, without batting an eyelid. However, not being able to think of any, I maintained a dignified silence.

Uncle kept on looking at us with a penetrating gaze. As far as I could recollect, my uncle had never interrogated hardened criminals, but should this contingency ever occur, I was certain he could reduce them to a sobbing bundle in a matter of minutes! While my face betrayed no signs of fear, from the waist down, I was more or less jellyfish. I fervently wished, at that moment, that I could slip into something more comfortable, like a concussion.

Uncle straightened up, his tone turning serious. "Alright then. You and Goldie will go to your own rooms and wait for me. I'll come to each of you—one at a time—and ask just one question."

It was one of those moments where you cough three times before you speak, but then decide not to say anything after all.

I looked at Goldie from the corner of my eye. He looked like he had just swallowed a rasgulla whose diameter he had underestimated by a wide margin.

I shrugged merrily and sauntered off. Goldie looked like his legs were made of lead; he made his way laboriously to his room.

I leaned close to Goldie and whispered reassuringly, "Don't worry, Goldie. Uncle's a pacifist"

Goldie blinked in confusion. "Meaning?"

There are days when I have the patience to deal with a poor vocabulary, but it wasn't one of those days!

"Meaning he'll *pass a fist* right across your stupid face." I muttered, giving Goldie a gentle shove. "Now off you go."

Uncle escorted Goldie first, leaving me alone in my room to anxiously wait out the silence. Seven long minutes later, the door creaked open, and Uncle stepped inside.

I sat up straight with an eager smile plastered on my face. "Oh yes, Uncle, you were going to ask me something?"

He nodded thoughtfully. "Ah, yes. You mentioned you experienced a tyre puncture, correct?"

"Yes, exactly!" I said earnestly. "Otherwise, we would've been home ages ago." I tried to look as innocent and helpful as possible.

"I see," Uncle said, narrowing his eyes just a little. "So—tell me, which tyre was punctured?"

I blinked. "Er, what?"

He folded his arms. "A car has four tyres, doesn't it? Which one was punctured?"

To cut a long story short, I have several happy memories of *pujo*, but this episode was not one of them!

Goldie Goes to a Picnic

This story unfolded when I had the misfortune of spending two weeks at my cousin Goldie's place. My readers are by now familiar with the name of Goldie. He was named Goldie, as you all know, because his mother (my aunt) thought he was pure and priceless like real gold, but we had established earlier that he was less gold and more goldfish material.

My aunt had invited us to her anniversary, so we packed our bags and went to stay at Goldie's place.

One afternoon, as I was sitting in Goldie's room, busy with my school work, a heavy weight descended on my toes, and the voice of Goldie polluted the room. The imbecile had decided to sit on the table where I was studying and, in his endeavour to do so, had squished my little toe. He was a certified klutz, and I doubt whether he could even walk across the Sahara without stumbling over something.

He seemed preoccupied and, to my utter dismay, started to recite some poetry that he had written:

'When she smiles — everything changes,
The sky also smiles, the stars are bright.
The world takes on a magical light.
The birds in the sky fly and sing,
And my dreams get a new wing!
She is like a sun — her radiance and her brightness.

And like a sunflower, I turn to her for happiness!'

Most of us who know Goldie well are aware that his journey through life is often impeded by a bunch of girls he easily becomes enamoured of, which often causes him great distress because the admiration is essentially one-sided. I did not ask him for whom he had written that piece of crap because I was well aware that, for the longest time, he had been infatuated with his neighbour, Aditi, who happened to be a good friend of mine.

The first objection I had to the above lines of poetry was that Goldie could never be compared to a sunflower. A cauliflower — why yes, certainly, there was a certain degree of resemblance, but certainly not to a sunflower. I told him so, and he gave me a dirty look. I really did not understand why he was so attracted to Aditi. She had big brown eyes and a chubby doll-like face, but she was not a perfectly pulchritudinous lady by any standards. However, boys will be boys, I suppose.

It appeared that Goldie had written tons of poetry for her and even joined yoga classes because Aditi also liked yoga. My aunt had even told me that, to become healthier, he had started drinking beet-carrot juice every morning (no doubt to impress Aditi)!

"Is this disgusting poem for Aditi?" I yawned.

He did not answer immediately, but his epidermis had flushed a rich pink, thereby confirming my suspicions.

"She's a nice girl, isn't she?" asked Goldie.

"Way out of your league, bro..." came the reply.

"Shut up!" Goldie snapped. "You've always been a pessimist. I like to look at the glass half full."

"For that," I retorted, "you need a half-filled glass. And as far as I'm concerned, yours is completely dry. Speaking of glasses being full — aren't you a bit too full of yourself lately?"

"I don't need your help with Aditi, okay?" Goldie huffed. "But, can you please at least help me join Sid Uncle's maths tuition?"

I gasped. Sid uncle was Aditi's father. Mr Siddharth Basu, a.k.a. Sid Uncle, was the most infamous and despised Maths professor in that '*paara*' (neighbourhood). Not only that, for a couple of years, my aunt had been begging him on to join Maths tuitions to improve his school grades, but he had always avoided her suggestions, like the plague.

I recalled my aunt telling him last year (and I quote her verbatim): "Goldie dear, tuitions are essential for improvement of your mind," and my readers are all aware that his mind could do with some improvement.

Doing some Maths myself, viz., adding two and two together, I could deduce the reasons for his sudden interest in Sid uncle's classes. Of course, he wanted to visit Aditi's home under the guise of being a student. His deceitful skulduggery did not fool me even for a second. How else could he strike up a friendship with Aditi?

Remember, it was the era before these frightful Facebook Friend Requests. Back then, if you liked a member of the opposite sex, you could do precious little apart from observing the object of your affection from a distance with a sedulous eye. Also, it would not behove a guy like Goldie to make a beeline for a neighbourhood girl like a hungry teenager charging into KFC and making a beeline for a Chicken Bucket.

I wondered whether I should help him. A part of my brain seemed to say: "Well, why should you? Has he ever helped you with anything? Has he ever given you anything apart from Chickenpox?" Another part of my brain said, "Well, why shouldn't you help him? If anything, he will owe you one, and you can force him to do your schoolwork, odd jobs, or even give you access to his secret stash of chocolates he has kept hidden in his cupboard. Also, if the contingency arises that Aditi ticks him off, you would be there to witness his downfall and tell the story."

It was a win-win situation. I decided to help him. The only hitch was Sid uncle!

Sid uncle was a tall and lanky, formidable-looking man with a shiny-domed head and huge caterpillar-like eyebrows. Although he was ostensibly a Maths Professor by daylight, he was the stuff of nightmares for most of his students.

If you looked at him closely, you would believe me when I say that God intended to create an eagle, but at the last minute, having changed His mind, opted to create another member of the species Homo sapiens. He looked exactly like an eagle with his piercing gaze and the claws (one claw, which was actually the nail on his little finger, was long and curved, and many of my neighbourhood pals had confided in me that he would poke his students with this claw if they failed to deliver him satisfactory results in his infamous Maths tests).

I said, "Okay, Goldie, I'll help you."

Like I had expected, this churned him up like an egg whisk. He brightened visibly and was going to say something, but I cut him short.

I said, "Listen, Uncle Sid will never like you because you are no good at Maths, and you are just the type of flippant and frivolous boy against whom he is very likely to be prejudiced."

They were bitter words, of course, describing one's own family, but well in keeping with his true character.

Goldie seemed hurt and said, "I am frivolous, am I?"

This was not a very snappy comeback as comebacks go, but wit was not one of Goldie's finer virtues.

I said, "Yes, to the core and what's more, Aditi is very good at Maths. So, if she finds out that you suck in her favourite subject, she will take your poetry and throw it on your face."

Goldie said nothing but sidled slowly out of the room, with an aching heart.

Well, to cut a long story short, I accompanied Goldie to Aditi's place the next evening to get him enrolled in Sid uncle's Maths tuition classes.

We sat meekly on the sofa in front of Sid Uncle. His eyes gleamed with that supercilious, penetrating gaze that had made him so very unpopular amongst his students. His moustache bristled menacingly, and his caterpillar-like eyebrows twitched ominously.

Sid uncle asked, "So, you are Goldie, eh?"

This question seemed to cover all the essential facts in question, so Goldie nodded excitedly.

Sid Uncle said, "You don't like Maths, do you? Or you failed in class and now need my help?"

Goldie stuttered, "N-no, sir, it's n-not that, I just need s-some help from you to improve my g-grades and my mother also wants that."

Sid uncle's lips curled. He could not have looked worse. He looked sinister enough with his lips in situ. Glaring at Goldie like he was amongst the lowest dregs of the underworld, he said, "Well, you can come on Sunday. I will assess your IQ first and then decide which of my batches would be suitable for you."

Goldie shuddered silently. "This Sunday, s-sir?"

Uncle Sid sneered, "No, the first Sunday next year. Of course, I mean this Sunday."

He could not have been glaring at Goldie with more obvious distaste if he had been a species belonging to the class Reptilia.

As a last act of bravado, Goldie extended his right hand and, with a conciliatory smile, said, "See you on Sunday, Sir."

Uncle Sid just gave an unpleasant grunt and said, "Well, if you don't have anything more to say, I'm going upstairs now to do my back exercises. I have tremendous lower back pain."

Feeling thankful that Sid uncle had his troubles too, we left the scene.

I totally sympathized with Goldie now. I knew that the coming Sunday would bring him as many tidings of great joy as stepping upon a raw crab. I could also understand the depths of his affection for Aditi. I mean, I would never willingly take tuition from Uncle Sid under any circumstances.

Anyway, Goldie continued his agonizing Maths tuition for about a week. Soon, it was time for Children's Day, and he would take out all his students for a picnic every year on Children's Day!

Goldie was beyond excited. It was the first time he would be going anywhere with Aditi. He urged me to go to Uncle

Sid's place the evening before the picnic and ask him whether he needed any help, and I grudgingly accepted.

Goldie, Aditi and I sat with Uncle Sid, and we were planning the finer details of the picnic.

"Let's play badminton," I suggested to Aditi.

"Of course," she said and wriggled from the base of her skull to her lumbo-sacral region with childish enthusiasm. I looked at Uncle Sid from the corner of my eye and found that he had a marked absence of childish enthusiasm in his demeanour. Goldie tried his best to infuse him with a bit of picnic spirit.

Goldie said, "Uncle, why don't we play cricket too? I heard you were quite the player in your childhood."

Uncle Sid eyed him coldly and said, "If you had as much interest in Maths as you do in this picnic, believe me, you'd be going places."

Goldie looked crestfallen at having been snubbed in front of Aditi.

Anyway, the next day dawned bright and sunny with a cool morning breeze. In short, it was a perfect day for a picnic. The picnic spot also proved to be, as predicted, a picnic spot — albeit a bit too crowded, for my liking. While I yield to no one in my appreciation of a good picnic spot — the greenery, the cacophony of kids tumbling down a slide, the sparkling banter amongst families and the occasional game of badminton/cricket, I had a premonition that something bad was going to happen.

We loafed around and chatted amongst ourselves while Goldie was trying to catch Aditi's attention, whenever he could. We played a few rounds of badminton and, after a while, sat down under a big shady tree, feeling hot.

We spotted a group of boys nearby, clustered around a middle-aged woman. The woman looked like Preity Zinta but was of surplus pounds. If you can just imagine Preity Zinta forgetting her diet and ingesting carbs and fatty acids generously for over a decade, you will get the picture. The boys chattered noisily as the aunty handed one ice cream after another to each of them.

Suddenly, Goldie sprinted towards Aditi and exclaimed, "Oh look, that lady over there is handing out free ice creams to everyone."

All of us turned towards Aunty like a bunch of bear cubs about to receive a pot of honey. This seemed too good to be true. Sure enough, a little boy with a gluttonous face walked up to that aunty, and she handed him a choco-bar! He walked away happily, making uncouth slurping noises, like a buffalo coming out of a swamp.

We looked excitedly at one another. There were around half a dozen boys, aged between 10 and 15, who had queued up near that aunty, and she was handing out ice cream cups/cones and hollering, "Okay, who's next? And which flavour for you, my dear?"

Aditi strode up confidently to her and shouted "strawberry" even before she could ask! Goldie stood right behind her like a faithful puppy.

Aunty stuttered, looking bewildered, "Er, what's your name, dear? Are you here with your parents?"

Aditi already had an arm outstretched, and on hearing these words, she withdrew her arm quickly. I do not know if you have ever seen a panther after it had its canines deeply embedded in a deer's throat, but if you were to disentangle the said deer from the afore-mentioned panther, you can imagine the look on the panther's face. Aditi's face had one such look, viz., she was piqued and justifiably so.

Now, Goldie, despite being as pronounced a fathead as ever existed in the eastern parts of the country, was a guy of impulse and hot-blooded impetuosity. Ever since Uncle Sid had snubbed him in front of Aditi the evening before, he had been silently fuming and brooding like a tormented soul. He was clearly looking for an outlet to vent steam, and it seemed that the Universe had handed this aunty on a platter to receive his pent-up venom.

Ergo, to save his object of affection from further humiliation, he drew himself to his full height and let her have it. I wanted to stop him, but I knew that when King Kong lets his fiery passion rise to the surface, there is almost no chance of passive remonstrance.

"That's not fair, aunty," he bellowed. "You are discriminating against her just because she's a girl. You gave ice-creams to so many boys before us, and just when a girl comes to you, she is questioned, even in this era of gender-equality! You, being a woman, should stand up for other women."

I cannot recall the exact words of the harangue, but I must say that it was a fine piece of oratory and continued for a good ten minutes. His speech ranged from the International Socialist women's conference in Copenhagen, which initially proposed Women's Day, to Indira Gandhi, our first woman Prime Minister! It would not be entirely out of order here to state that Goldie had surpassed himself, and the look that he gave aunty was a look which had a thousand silent expletives!

Uncle Sid, hearing the commotion, had sidled up silently to the mob scene and looked like he had been hit in the solar plexus with a dumbbell.

Meanwhile, the ice-cream-aunty, who was hitherto smiling affably, looked like she had just woken up from a deep slumber and found herself hugging a python. There were some gasping-like noises emanating from her vocal cords,

which presumably meant she would have liked to have the floor earlier, but if she had asked me, I would have told her it was useless! You can't switch off Goldie when he is blurting out a speech so passionately, even if you try your best.

I gave a sidelong glance at Aditi. There was an unmistakable look of reverence in her eyes.

Finally, Auntie shook her head vehemently and stuttered, "No, no, no, my dear, not at all. Listen, I only gave them ice cream because they are my nephews, you see. I have nothing against girls, my dear."

Goldie looked like he had been struck by lightning. How long he remained motionless like a finished product by a taxidermist, I do not know. I have said it before, and I will say it again: wherever Goldie went, he invited chaos and ruin, and there was an almost creative ingenuity in the ways he did it.

Uncle Sid did not say anything but snorted like a rhino at the water trough!

Anyway, the time was ripe for me to pitch in. It seemed cousinly to save Goldie from apoplexy! I quickly apologized to aunty, on his behalf and tried to hand over some candies and a few packets of chips to her beastly nephews as a way of offering an olive branch.

Goldie tried to say something, but he looked like a lamb that had a leaf stuck in its larynx. He uttered some non-committal, incoherent words like a child with a cleft palate, mumbling something. It can never be too pleasant for a guy who had risen to the occasion like an alpha male to change his stance to ignoble apologies. His face looked flushed. Either the beet juice that he had been consuming had imparted that ugly vermilion colour to his cheeks, or his red blood corpuscles had risen to the surface in embarrassment!

The plump aunty walked away slowly (in any case, she was built for stability and not for speed) from the scene, looking a bit listless, viz., not so much bounce per ounce anymore.

Uncle Sid glared at Goldie, but thankfully, did not say anything right there. I had an ugly premonition that Goldie was about to receive a surprise Maths test in his next class, which he could never pass without strategic cheating on a massive scale.

There was no point in waiting there anymore. It was clearly an episode fraught with embarrassing potentialities. Thus, strategic retreat was the only course to pursue, and we all scattered away in different directions.

I looked at Goldie. He had stopped prancing around like a cheerful bunny, and his movements were more akin to the surreptitious prowling of a thief, with his spinal cord tying itself into knots frequently.

Only Aditi had a beatific smile on her face, and from that day onward, she became friends with Goldie.

Summer Vacation with Goldie

It was the beginning of my month-long summer vacation. My aunt had invited me over to stay with her for a week. Usually, I would have politely declined, but I had been informed that her son, Goldie (my cousin), had recently returned from New York. I knew he had brought a lot of imported chocolates with him, and as a glutton, I needed to have my share. In a middle-class family, if someone goes to New York on vacation, it usually means they have relatives there. Goldie's distant cousin lived there, and he had gone to stay with them. Anyway, I had to go and grab my share of the chocolates because asking Goldie to give up his chocolates for me was like asking Dracula to give up drinking his share of the blood. So, I headed to my aunt's house, muttering to myself, "Lead me not into temptation, because I already know the way."

Now, let's start with the basics. My cousin Goldie was around 17 then (2 years older than me). He was named Goldie because his mother (my aunt) thought he was pure and priceless like real gold. The truth is, my aunt just loved gold jewellery and couldn't get enough of it (for her, anything that glitters is gold).

In my opinion, Goldie was less of gold and more of goldfish material. He was always seen in a monkey cap in winter. Monkey caps and names like Goldie are ways devised by Bengali mothers to ward off members of the opposite sex from their sons. Anyway, Goldie was his parents' favourite child. (He was also the only child, so there's that, of course).

He was so dumb that if you spoke to him for ten minutes, you would wonder why no one had hit him with a brick yet. Or maybe you would realise why people put how-to-use directions on a bottle of shampoo. He was that weirdo who said strange stuff like 'head west' while giving directions and said more dumb things before 11 am than most people did in their lifetimes. I could not handle him even if he came with instructions. In a nutshell, this Goldie had no silver lining, but he was living proof that God has a sense of humour too.

Now, suddenly, after returning from New York, I noticed that he had drastically changed. He said weird things like "I'm allergic to pollen..." and his conversation was generously peppered with "bro..." "whatcha..." "whateva…" etc.

Previously, whenever his mother cooked a delicacy and asked him how it was while eating, he would just grunt something incomprehensible, but now, he actually complimented her on the "rich texture and flavours" of the gravy that she cooked. He was getting more and more suspicious each day.

He also got unusually excited about mundane things like the weather, a TV show, or a book. He would suddenly say things like, "It's a beautiful morning, isn't it?"

Well, I don't like morning people (or mornings or even people, actually), so I grumbled while he went about the house with a silly grin splashed across his face.

I wished he had gone to London instead of New York. The British were grey and miserable about everything (just like their weather) and didn't have this obnoxious need to be gleefully smiling all the time.

I asked my aunt one day, "Have you noticed a change in Goldie ever since he returned from New York?"

"Hmm, there's a subtle change, maybe, hardly noticeable," she agreed.

"Subtle? Yes, it is hardly noticeable, just like the pandemic!" I said.

One morning, I chanced upon his personal diary. I wanted to see if he had written anything about me, so I browsed through it. Anyway, the only thing he wrote about me was that I had boundary issues and I didn't respect other people's privacy. (I wonder why!)

Nevertheless, I found out that he had a crush on his neighbour, a girl called Aditi. That explained the goofy look on his face and his newfound penchant for good weather, music and poetry. Now, Aditi and I have been friends since childhood. She shared a common terrace with my aunt, and we would sometimes play together on the terrace and make fun of Goldie together.

He had written some pretty mushy and nauseating stuff about Aditi. I could not resist the urge to scribble in his diary. I knew he would be mad at me when he saw my scribbling, but er... that was the idea!

(Whatever I scribbled, I am writing within brackets.)

Dear Aditi,

You are so beautiful. God has truly made all things so beautiful.

(He has made you, too, Goldie, and also the platypus, but never mind.)

You cause happiness wherever you go.

(And you, whenever you go.)

Life is good.

(You should get one.)

Now that you are in my life.

If you ask anyone, you will know that I'm different. My parents say that I am a treasure.

(Such a treasure that we want to bury you.)

I have recently represented Bengalis in the 'Bengalis have talent' show as well.

(Er, which other community could you represent?)

Everything in my life is going well.

(You have obviously overlooked a great many things.)

I know you like yoga, Aditi, and I have also started practising it. Now, I feel that I am in good shape.

(Good shape for a circle, you mean?)

I believe that people should inspire each other to become the best version of themselves.

(You would be in perfect shape if you ran as much as your pen.)

I believe in love, Aditi, and I also believe in marriage. Do you know why God wants people to get married?

(It is because He doesn't want their awful day to end at work.)

If you ever came into my life, there's only one word to describe it.

(Imagination?)

True love

(That's two words, silly.)

Yours and mine would be a match made in heaven.

(Yes, by a retarded Cupid.)

Tell me, Aditi, what would you look for in a relationship with me?

(A way out?)

I don't want to end up like my uncle Swarup.

(That's true, he had two marriages, but both were unfortunate. His first wife left him, and his second one didn't.)

He is always sad and never smiles. You make me smile. I'm writing all my true feelings here. A personal diary never lies, you know.

(And lucky for you, it doesn't laugh.)

You are really like a queen. And what's a queen without a king?

(Technically, more powerful.)

I don't know anything about love, my dear.

(They say ignorance is bliss, but I find yours rather disturbing.)

I only know that I will love you forever.

People say that one can be whoever one wants to be in life.
(But in your case, you shouldn't aim too high.)

With time, you will also love me, I'm sure. Time is the best teacher.

(But it kills all its students, right?)'

I heard Goldie coming up the stairs, and I quickly put down his diary and fled the scene.

He came to my room after 20 minutes and looked at me suspiciously.

He asked, "Hey, where were you between 4 and 5?"

"Kindergarten," I replied without thinking.

Goldie rolled his eyes. "No, I mean between 4 pm and 5 pm?"

"Oh, here only," I said, shrugging.

He leaned in a bit. "Hey, listen, whatcha doin'?"

"Umm, wasting my life," I answered dryly.

Goldie laughed. "Ha ha, no, no. I mean, today evening?"

"Er, nothing," I admitted.

"Why don't all of us go to a nearby café?" he suggested. "You, me, and a deity."

"Which deity?" I asked, confused.

He smirked. "Aditi, yaa."

"Then lose the fake accent, *na,*" I shot back.

I decided to help the poor fellow. I agreed to go to the café with them. We got ready to go out.

"What's that smell?" I asked, scrunching up my nose.

"That's my deo," Goldie announced proudly. "Why? Is the smell bad?"

"No, but must you marinate yourself in it? Aditi can probably smell you through these walls. And why are you wearing that awful green shirt?"

He looked down at himself. "Why? Is it that ugly?"

"Yes. That's why it complements your face," I said before continuing, "Anyway, listen, there are two ways to woo women."

Goldie suddenly perked up, interested.

"But neither of them works," I concluded, bursting into loud laughter.

He glared. "Why do you go out of your way to piss me off?"

"Believe me," I said with a shrug, "it's not out of my way at all."

"Do you suffer from an urge to be sarcastic?" he asked.

"No, I don't suffer at all," I replied cheerfully. "I actually enjoy it."

Goldie frowned. "Why aren't you ready? And why are you putting one grape after another into your mouth?"

"Because I can't do the same with watermelons," I said. "Are you always this annoying, or are you putting in a special effort today?"

He ignored that. "You know, Aditi has invited me to her yoga class too. What do you think I should wear?"

"A T-shirt that says, 'I don't belong here.'" I suggested.

"Well, I don't agree with you," he huffed.

"That's okay," I replied. "I can't force you to be right."

Goldie folded his arms. "I think you should apologise to me."

"Alright," I said with mock sincerity, "I'm sorry for the rude, insulting, and accurate things I have said."

Goldie was seething. He took out his pen from his shirt pocket. At first, I thought that he was going to stab me with it, but he pointed it at me and croaked hoarsely, "There's a devil at the end of this pen."

"Which end?" I asked.

Anyway, after our endless banter, we went to the café. Aditi told us that it was her birthday that Saturday. So, I told Goldie that he must give her a gift on Friday, at midnight.

My uncle and aunt were early sleepers, and I could keep a watch while Goldie tip-toed to the terrace to meet Aditi. Aditi hesitated initially but eventually agreed.

At 11:50 pm on Friday, I surreptitiously tip-toed to the stairway and saw that the coast was clear. Apart from my uncle's soft snores, there was absolute silence. I saw Goldie walking with a torch and the huge, ugly pink teddy that he had purchased for Aditi. For some reason, he was wearing his ghastly monkey cap, even though it was only November.

He looked at me, and I gave him the green signal, a thumbs-up.

He tip-toed up the stairs, but unfortunately, the clumsy ass stubbed his toe on a potted plant near the stairs and staggered. The torch fell from his hands and clanked noisily. I couldn't see anything in the dark.

Suddenly, I heard my uncle's voice shouting, *"Chor... Chor..."*

I couldn't hear Goldie. Only some incomprehensible muffled noises could be heard.

In another minute, my aunt had woken up and switched on the lights. The crime scene was now bathed in light.

To my horror, I saw that my uncle had grabbed Goldie from behind and had put his large fist across his mouth. Poor Goldie could not talk. I could only hear his muffled sobs. Since he was wearing a monkey cap, his face was not visible, and he was also wearing pink shorts (which were presumably new, since I had never seen them before). Naturally, my uncle had presumed that a thief had broken in.

Finally, Goldie wriggled out of my uncle's steely embrace and braced his parents.

"Goldie? What are you doing?" Uncle's voice boomed from behind us.

"N–n–nothing." Goldie stammered. "I just wanted to go to the terrace for some fresh air."

Aunty narrowed her eyes. "And what are you wearing?"

I stepped in helpfully. "They're called shorts. Like pants, essentially, but much shorter."

Uncle pointed sternly. "And what are you doing with a teddy bear?"

It was fun to see Goldie stuttering. Anyway, I came to his rescue.

"It was actually a surprise gift for you, Aunty," I explained quickly. "Your anniversary is around the corner, *na*. So I told Goldie to buy you a present and hide it on the terrace."

Anyway, all is well that ends well. Not surprisingly, after that night, Goldie has never worn a monkey cap again.

The Adventures of My Aunt - Mishti Mashi

Mishti Mashi and the Rock Concert

I was around 17 years old then. My cousin Taniya (2 years younger than me) and I were very excited as Pitbull was coming to India (Noida) to perform. I knew this was my only chance to see him perform live on stage. I convinced my parents to let Taniya and me go to Noida for one day. Unfortunately, they allowed us only under one condition — either my mother or my aunt (Taniya's mother — Mishti Mashi) would accompany us.

Mishti Mashi was only too glad to oblige. I was crestfallen. For those of you who have read my earlier story, you will know that my aunt, Mishti Mashi, was an insufferable chatterbox. It wasn't that I hated her; let's just say I wasn't particularly excited about her existence.

On the day of the concert, Mashi woke us up at the crack of dawn. She seemed unnaturally ebullient as she pushed us out of bed.

"Tell me, what inspires you to get out of bed every morning?" she asked gleefully.

"Umm, mostly my bladder," I mumbled in my sleep.

"No, no, no, you must wake up happy every morning."

Later on, I realised that it was not her excitement to see Pitbull that motivated her to wake us up at the crack of dawn. No, sir, it was because she did not want us to miss the free breakfast buffet. She kept urging us to stuff ourselves to our gills and reminding us that breakfast was the most important meal of the day. Also, to my horror, I saw her sneaking muffins and apples from the breakfast buffet and stuffing them in her purse! However, her purse was like the Bermuda triangle — the stuff that goes in can never be seen again. So I knew that she would take the stolen goods back home. I remembered the one time on my birthday, when she gifted me at least 3 dozen tea sachets she had collected from different hotels she had been to. However, I took comfort in the fact that she was not all that bad — at least she did not nick the life-jacket from the aircraft.

We took a shared cab along with two Punjabi teenagers to reach the said concert. One of them was giving directions to the driver, *"Arrey uncle ji, otthe lo otthe lo."* Mashi whispered in my ear, "The driver's name is Othello? My God, do you think he is a fan of Shakespeare?"

I shushed her and implored her to keep quiet.

We reached the venue of the concert at least an hour before and waited with bated breath for Pitbull. Mashi had worn a bright orange silk saree. She reminded me of a multi-coloured parakeet. She whispered in my ear, "I hope I don't look too out of place."

I looked at the crowd of teenagers around me in frayed denims. Oh yes, she blended in just fine, like maple syrup in Mutton Biryani.

Soon enough, Pitbull made a grand entry to deafening cheering and hooting. The crowd went berserk. The girls swooned and danced to earth-shattering music. Pitbull was wearing a hoodie, and his face was half-hidden. Mashi did not seem at all impressed. She looked at me with a dung-under-the-nose expression and hissed, "How do you know it's Mr Bull? We can't even see his face, for all you know, it can be a look-alike."

I shouted into her ear, "His name is not Mr. Bull, it's Pitbull—one word. And of course it's him, you'll see."

She still did not seem convinced and, much to my chagrin, kept on asking really lame questions, like "Has he always

been bald? How can a celebrity be bald? My mother always asked us to use coconut oil every day, you see. It prevents hair fall."

I looked at her well-oiled hair. Yes, even Oman could not boast of so much oil, I suppose.

Anyway, Pitbull was dishing out my favourite songs, and I stopped talking to her.

She interrupted me again. "I only have a few words to say. I don't think he sings that well."

I also had a few words for her, viz. 'I think you need help.' However, I chose to maintain a dignified silence, partly out of courtesy but mostly because she had paid for the concert tickets.

After around 30 minutes of hooting and cheering, we were very thirsty. A guy was handing out mineral water bottles inside the auditorium. Mashi yelled at the top of her voice, "*Dada, arrey oh dada, eedhaar, eedhaar.*"

The guy glared at her and said, "Madam ji, *dada kisko bol rahi hai?*"

"*Arrey, na, na,* dada means brother in Bengali, don't mind."

As soon as Mashi heard the price of mineral water, she literally screamed. "Rs 350 for Bisleri?" she asked him, aghast. "Do you know, we used to do our entire Puja shopping for 350/- when we were kids?"

The boy gave her a withering look and walked away. She then told me that she had a brainwave — we should drink Coke instead of water (because she had seen at the food counter that a bottle of Coke was priced at 100 bucks). She looked around at the other kids who thronged us. There was a guy standing next to us — a Caucasian male, aged about 17.

He was skinny and had tattoos all over his arms. Half his head was shaved, and the other half was covered with spiky purple hair. His eyes were closed and he was swaying gently to the music.

Mishti Mashi whispered to me, "Is he sleeping?"

I wanted to tell her, "No, he is training to die", but I restrained myself and told her, "Why don't you ask him?"

She nudged him softly and asked him, "Hello, do you know if Coke is available?"

The boy turned to her and looked at her with glazed, half-opened eyes. He resembled a lobotomised rock.

"Coke?" he asked, blinking his eyes.

"Yes, Coke," she replied. Then, in a desperate bid to sound cool, she added, "I am totally into Coke, you see."

The boy looked at her incredulously and mumbled, "No, man, I dunno about Coke, never taken that stuff. I'm into pot. That's the real shit."

Mashi turned to me and hissed, "He has never had Coke? Do you believe that? And why is he talking about shit in public? Really, kids these days are totally shameless."

She decided to go out and buy the Coke herself from the food counter. I looked at the excessively long queue at the food counter. From where I was standing, it looked like the queue stretched from Noida right across Haryana and Punjab and must have reached all the way to Lahore. I implored her not to go, but my words were about as useful as the 'queue' in queue.

She told me in an assertive voice, "Listen, I am still young, I can do it. One can only be young once."

(Yes, one can only be young once, but one can be stupid forever...) I shrugged and let her go.

Thankfully, we did not see her again till the end of the concert. After the concert ended, she emerged, victorious, with a small bottle of Coke in her hand. She was jostling her way into the auditorium and yelling at the top of her voice, "*Arrey meri choti nahi meel raaha hai...meri choti...*"

(*Choti* means slippers in Bengali and Ponytail in Hindi).

All the folks gathered around her, looking quizzically at each other, and I saw one girl gesturing to another, 'her screw is loose or what?'

I waited until the commotion cleared and walked up to her. By then, she had all but forgotten about her slippers and was talking animatedly to a Punjabi lady, "*Arrey,* imagine they didn't even give us a food packet or cold drinks. Do you know how much we paid for the tickets? If I tell my mother that we came all the way from Kolkata to see that bald man sing, she will faint. At least two shingaras and a *mishti* would be okay."

I marvelled at her ability to talk incessantly to anyone, anywhere. I think the amount of time taken by a whale to give birth must be less than the time that she spends talking daily. The lady that she was talking to seemed flummoxed, but there was no stopping my *mashi.*

Mashi politely asked her whether she had ever visited Bengal and whether she knew Bengali.

The lady shook her head and replied, "No, I don't know Bengali. But everything sounds like *Esho, Bosho, Haansho* — all *sho sho,* right?"

(C'mon, lady, if I had a coin for every smart thing you just said, I'd still be broke... For sho...)

Trying to keep the conversation moving, Mashi complimented her children and asked their names.

"They're Sweety and Lovely," the lady announced proudly, "and my son is Honey."

Mashi smiled and responded, "Oh, *acchha*! My daughter's name is Taniya, but her *daak naam*—nickname—is Puchki."

"Puchki?" the lady frowned. "But that's something they eat in Kolkata, right?"

"No, no!" Mashi corrected her, slightly exasperated. "That's *phuchka*! *Aah moron.*"

(*"Aah moron"* is a Bengali expression, like saying "Oh my God.")

The lady gasped, offended. "Moron? Madam ji, please mind your language! How can you call me a moron?"

I butted in quickly and clarified the matter to the best of my abilities, before a cat-fight could ensue.

On catching sight of me and Taniya, she waved at us. "You know what would be good now?"

("Your absence", I muttered under my breath, but she didn't hear me).

Mashi rubbed her ears dramatically. "*Uff,* all that noise has made my ears buzz," she complained. "I think I'll meditate today. You know, I'm actually very good at meditation."

(Isn't it only natural? Given your level of intelligence, the state of absolute thoughtlessness must come naturally to you.)

Her banter continued throughout the journey, right up to the airport, "*Arrey,* all these kids nowadays *na* — no *kaalture* — what clothes they are wearing! Torn jeans! And what names these people have here in Delhi! Sweety, Lovely, Honey. *Arrey,* Bengali names are much better. My mother's name was Shaagota-lokkhi. What a beautiful name and you call this deafening music good? *Arrey,* Bengalis are good singers like Kishore Kumar, Kumar Sanu."

She only stopped talking when both Taniya and I firmly shut our eyes and pretended to sleep.

Mishti Mashi and Blondie

I was a medical student at the time and had to go to Delhi for an entrance exam. For some reason, my parents thought I was responsible enough to become a doctor but not responsible enough to travel to Delhi alone. Go figure! And who would chaperone me to Delhi? Yes, all of you have guessed it – my Mishti Mashi (MM).

I still remember her scurrying up to the boarding-pass counter, elbowing everyone and trying to jump the queue. One irate gentleman stopped her and said, "Madam, I am waiting in the queue..."

"Sorry, I have a flight to catch," she said breathlessly and brushed past him.

(Yes, you are the only one who has a flight to catch; everyone else just comes to picnic at the airport.)

Even during the flight, she was an insufferable chatterbox. Much to my chagrin, she started giving me unending advice. The conversation was mainly one-sided, as I did not voice most of my remarks and maintained a stony-faced exterior. Excerpts of this million-dollar conversation are as follows:

MM started, "I know that this phase of your life must be difficult, so much to study, the pressure of exams, but remember, this too shall pass."

I nodded politely while a voice in my head muttered, *"Yes, it is passing… like a kidney stone right now. Thanks to you."*

"Always be grounded. You know what happens to people who keep their feet firmly fixed to the ground, *na*?"

(Er, they have trouble putting on their pants.)

"Success and failure are not exactly like life and death; if you don't succeed at first, keep trying again and again."

(Hope the pilot flying this aircraft does not follow this.)

"My parents always told me that life is not about fixing problems, sometimes we should start over and create something new."

(Now I know why her parents opted for a second child after her.)

Sensing my mood, she asked, "*Uff*, why are you wearing your grumpy hat today? And why are you continuously yawning?"

(Oh, not only the hat, I have the whole outfit on with matching socks. And I only yawn when I am very interested, please continue.)

Finally, she exclaimed angrily, "You're not saying anything."

I wanted to say that 'No response IS a response and a very powerful one at that,' but I didn't mean to push all her buttons; I was just looking for the 'mute' one.

Finally, she got bored and started chatting with a co-passenger, seated beside her – a middle-aged Caucasian, blonde woman.

MM: "Hello, what is your name? Where are you going?"

I hissed into her ear, "This flight is going to Delhi, isn't it?" but she paid no heed to me.

Blondie: "Oh, hi, I'm Megan. Well, I'm backpacking across India extensively and will go to Rajasthan after Delhi. I love the rich history associated with these places. What about you?"

MM: "I am going to Delhi with my niece, she has an exam there. We will stay there with my younger sister, Bulu. She has a son named Goldie, and he loves me very much. Goldie is such a sweetheart; he is just like pure gold."

I was drinking water and I nearly choked. Sweetheart? Goldie was less of gold and more of goldfish material, and he was so dumb that if you spoke to him, you would realise why people put how-to-use directions on a bottle of shampoo.

MM: "Someday he will go very far, my Goldie."

(Yes, and I hope he stays there.)

Blondie seemed to be intrigued by MM. Probably, she hadn't met anyone like her before.

Blondie: "So, you like travelling?"

MM: "Oh, I love travel; my hobby is backpacking across Europe."

This time, I actually choked on the water. Come on, everyone has a right to tell a white lie or two, but backpacking across Europe! Did she even know what 'backpacking' meant? She had never even set foot outside the country!

The only instance of backpacking that I could think of was the time she carried a bagful of books from College Street to Kanchrapara.

Blondie: "Oh, how lovely, I am planning to go backpacking too, maybe to the south coast of Italy next year."

MM: "Oh, that's so nice. I would like to go there too someday."

Really? I wanted to tell her that the maximum that she could afford was the west coast of India, viz. Goa, but I maintained a dignified silence.

Blondie: "My journey started with Bali, y'know, 'cos I just wanted to find myself."

MM: "Well, you should visit Chandni Chowk in Delhi; you will never find yourself there, nor will anyone else, ha ha ha."

Saying this, she guffawed so loudly that several passengers turned their heads to look at her.

MM: "You know I love beaches." then, turning towards me, she added, "Hey, tell her about your birthday party that I had planned...at the beach in Puri, *na*."

I shuddered. It was the most traumatising birthday ever. We were at Puri, and it was MM's brilliant idea to cut the cake on the beach. It was a windy day. A gust of wind blew out the candles before I could, and the second gust got some sand in my eye. I rubbed my eye so hard that my contact lens fell off. Due to my high myopia, I could not see anything and nearly chopped off my father's finger as he tried to help me cut the cake. Then, all of us huddled together, stony-faced and ate the cake à la carte, while I played Helen Keller at the beach.

Blondie: "Have you ever travelled alone? I love solo travel."

MM: "No, I haven't, but I am very street smart."

I got a crick in my neck from shaking my head in disbelief. I do not know which street she was referring to – there was a *Gadha* (donkey) road in Jalandhar as far as I knew.

By now, MM was very pleased with Blondie, because she opened her purse and offered her some cheese that she had nicked from the breakfast buffet at the airport. Her penchant for anything free/complimentary was well-known in our family. In fact, if she ever wrote an autobiography, it would be titled, 'Who moved my free cheese?'

MM: "Please have this cheese, it's lovable."

"Lovely, not lovable," I hissed into her ears.

Blondie: "Oh, I can't, I'm vegan."

MM: "But you said you are Megan."

I couldn't take it anymore. I budged in.

"Why don't you share your tiffin, *mashi*?"

I wanted to get rid of the ghastly poha that she had packed for us to eat during the flight.

MM: "Oh, yes, please have this. It is poha, pure veg food." She beamed as she took out the tiffin box and extended it to her newfound friend.

Blondie: "What is poh-hah?"

MM: *"Cheerer pulao...er...maney...poha...mane...ki j boli."*

It was kind of hilarious trying to watch her put her entire vocabulary in one sentence. Anyway, I came to her rescue after she stuttered for around 3 minutes, because she was family, after all, and family must help each other or whatever. Besides, having watched all the episodes of MasterChef, I was an expert in this field.

I said, "Oh, you know, poha, just flattened rice flakes with the rich flavours of Indian herbs, slow cooked with sautéed onions and a dash of lime, garnished with basil and coriander."

All the passengers stood up and gave me a standing ovation. (Of course, they didn't. Come on, don't believe everything I write, guys).

MM beamed at me. Blondie took a spoonful, and we waited with bated breath.

Now, cooking was not one of her finer skills. I remember the one time she had cooked mutton biryani. The mutton pieces were so undercooked that probably a skilled vet could have saved the goat. However, Blondie seemed to like the taste and even appreciated her culinary skills.

MM started boasting as usual, "Oh, I love cooking, but I have so many interests, you know. I am very, very modern."

Blondie looked at her incredulously. She did not look the 'modern' type at all. In fact, in her crisp cotton saree, she looked every bit of the *pavitra Bharatiya naari* with the Aloknath seal of approval.

Blondie: "Oh, I'm so tired, you know, I haven't slept properly last night. Just wanna crash now."

I do not know what happened after that, but MM became totally quiet. The eerie silence intrigued me, and I asked her why she was so quiet. She replied, looking scared, "Why does she want us to crash? Do you think she is a suicide bomber?"

I hushed her up and explained that the word 'crash' meant to sleep, but she did not buy my theory.

Anyway, I enjoyed the rest of the journey in blissful silence.

Mishti Mashi Attends a Wedding

It was the first year of my marriage. I married into a Marwadi family, and we were all geared up for the winter wedding of a distant cousin. In my experience, weddings have the same effect on Marwadis as a full moon does on werewolves. In other words, they go berserk. Most probably, one-fourth of the entire Marwadi population was invited to this wedding, and they even invited my folks, viz, my father, grandmother and aunts.

While most of my folks declined politely, my aunt, Mishti Mashi, readily agreed to go! I was flummoxed. While she was as sweet as her name, she happened to be an insufferable chatterbox and lacked a very important trait, viz., tact.

We went to the wedding, all decked up. Not to be outdone by the Marwadi ladies, my Mishti Mashi had come fully prepared. She looked like a model of P.C. Chandra. I think she had worn all the jewellery that she had. She beamed at me, all excited, in a multi-coloured saree, looking like a colourful parakeet. I had worn a lehenga to blend in with the crowd (pic below), but in vain. Most of the guests looked at me and Mishti Mashi like we were migratory birds of an exotic variety.

The wedding scene was dazzling and glittering — it did not seem entirely impossible for an aircraft to seriously mistake it for a runaway and land bang on top of us. Mishti Mashi seemed all excited like a little girl, and her incessant chatter had already started.

The groom's grandfather had passed away recently, and we were greeted at the entrance of the banquet hall by an elderly gentleman. To my utter chagrin, Mashi exclaimed, *"Oh, apni achhen? Ami toh bhablam apni gechen."* (Oh, you are alive? I thought you had passed away.)

I turned red like a beetroot and hissed into her ear that this gentleman was someone else. Thankfully, that chap's knowledge of Bengali was nothing to write home about, and he did not understand a word she had uttered.

Thereafter, we went to meet the bride and were ushered in by her father. He greeted us with a cursory, *"Arrey, itna late se aaye aaplog… ugli function mein jaldi aana hai."*

Mashi did not quite catch the finer essence of what he said. Nevertheless, she pounced on the opportunity to budge in and talk: *"Arrey, ugly function ekdom nahi; khoob pretty function; shob kichhu bahut pretty aur beautiful hai, aap peeta hai?"*(There is nothing ugly about the function; everything is so pretty and beautiful. Are you the father?)

(She meant *pita/pitaji*/father; in her heavily accented Hindi, she had said *peeta* instead of *pita*.)

The entire Marwadi clan stared at her in horror. Asking the father of the bride about his drinking habits in full view of all the guests was generally frowned upon, as evidenced by the horrified looks on their faces.

The bride's father firmly declined, *"Arrey main bilkul bhi nahi peeta,"* while his wife gave him suspicious looks.

I quickly clarified the matter, and a wave of relief seemed to wash over them all.

Before I could catch my breath, Mishti Mashi had asked the bride, "What is your name, *beti*?"

She replied, "Suman."

"Shumon?" She looked at me incredulously and whispered a bit too loudly for comfort. *"Shumon toh chheleder naam, na?"* (Suman is a name for boys, *na*?)

I found it ironic that she should comment on anyone's name, given that her parents had named her Mishti. Since her surname was Dey, her full name was Mishti Dey (in Bengali, it means 'give me *mishti*/sweets'). I often wondered whether her parents were sadists. Come on, guys, her name was Mishti Dey; she obviously had a troubled life.

After the preliminary round of introduction, the conversation shifted to the bride's trousseau.

The mother of the bride was gleefully talking about her daughter's bridal lehenga, by Sabyasachi, worth Rs. 1 lakh! Mashi seemed flabbergasted and whispered in my ear, asking me whether the same lehenga would be worn by the other brides in the family too. I hissed into her ears, "Nooo", and begged her to stop talking.

Throwing caution to the wind, she continued, "*Arrey*, I also like brands. You know, I wear only branded things. I always wear Hush Puppies shoes." She mispronounced 'hush' as 'whoosh', which created some confusion, but she cleared it soon enough — taking off her oversized sandals and brandishing it in full view, like swatting a fly. Jabbing a finger at the 'Hush Puppy' logo, she asked triumphantly, "See?"

Everyone looked at each other in horrified silence.

She continued, "Only branded things! Also, my husband only wears shirts of...of..."

She seemed to have temporary amnesia and turned to me.

"Oi brand ta ki re? Hussain bole ki ekta..." (What is that brand?

Named after Hussain?)

"Zakir Hussain?" I asked disbelievingly.

It seemed highly improbable that the tabla maestro had branded shirts named after him.

Suman (the bride) cut in, "Oh, you mean Van Heusen? That's van hew-zen, not Hussain."

Mashi replied, beaming, "*Oi heushen hussain ek ee holo.* Potato, poh-tah-to, ha ha ha. Have you read Shakespeare?"

"Yes, aunty," Suman replied meekly, "actually I had English Honours in college."

Mashi said, "Oh! You studied Literature? Only the rich study Literature."

Then, glancing at me from the corner of her eyes (I was looking daggers at her), she said, "Shakespeare only said na... What's in a name? Imagine if your in-laws ask you your name, don't say, 'What's in a name, beti?' Ha ha ha."

She laughed so hard at her own joke that her eyes teared up. Her laughter was famous in our family. It sounded like a cross between a hyena's laughter and the cry of a wounded dog. She seemed to give a totally new dimension to 'laugh like no one is watching, sing like no one is listening, or whatever.' (She also drove like there was no one on the road, but that's a different story, not for today.)

She continued, relentlessly, "And what is this thee thou business? Why couldn't Shakespeare write in plain English? I always thought only a chap high on *ganja* can write like that, ha ha ha."

Her laughter was greeted by stony silence. I rolled my eyes so hard that I am sure a few guests must have thought that I had been having an epileptic fit. The bride's eyebrows were raised so high that they had a risk of disappearing permanently into her hairline.

The bride's mother cut in, "Mishti ji, you are looking very nice and different in this saree."

"*Arrey, tai toh,* I know I don't look a Bengali at all. In fact, people often ask me whether I am a north-Indian."

I stared at her in disbelief. She looked about as Bengali as *Jharna Ghee* or *Dulaler Taal Mishri* to me.

An aged gentleman approached the periphery, and, in an attempt to divert the conversation, I went up to him and touched his feet, only to be interrupted by the bride's family: "*Arrey,* he is Ram Dayal, our servant."

I looked at him sheepishly while he kept on ogling at me and patting my head (a bit too enthusiastically) and peppered the conversation with "*Jeetey raho, bitiya*" and so on and so forth.

I took Mishti Mashi to a corner and asked her to lie low for a while, though even Mount Everest would do a better job at lying low than her, at that point in time. However, she promised me that she would be inconspicuous from then on and not talk too much.

Soon enough, the groom entered the scene on horseback. The horse looked colossal, like it had just galloped out of *The Lord of the Rings,* while the groom was a skinny, prematurely balding guy who was holding onto the horse with his dear life!

As soon as Mishti Mashi saw the groom, she started yelling "*Ullullulululu*" at the top of her voice, so much for being inconspicuous.

The groom looked frightened and clung onto the horse lest it start galloping away like a war-horse (her *ullullululu* did sound like a war-cry).

I wanted to sink into the floor and disappear. I looked around. There was stunned silence. Someone in the crowd asked, *"Daura pada hai kya*? "Nobody could understand the *banshee*-like cry at the entry of the groom.

"Arrey, ulu dao, ulu dao," she kept on urging the guests.

(This is a common ritual in Bengali weddings.)

One of the groom's brothers shouted, *"Ullu*? *Kisko ullu bol rahi hai yaar*?"

There was utter chaos, and I was at my wits' end.

Thankfully, the cameraman and his crew came to our rescue. The bride and groom were ushered onto the stage while I caught Mishti Mashi by the elbow and steered her away from the scene of the crime towards the buffet.

Ever since I was a child, I've always seen her make a beeline for the buffet at every wedding. So, I was suitably perplexed as to why she was neglecting the gastronomic delights that evening. On rigorous enquiry, she confessed sheepishly that in Bengali weddings, she usually jostled her way to the Biryani counter at the earliest opportunity, lest all the mutton pieces were polished off from the biryani by the ravenous guests, leaving only the sorry-looking rice sans mutton. However, as veg biryani was the entrée, she did not feel the need to dive headfirst into the buffet.

I left her at the snacks counter and found a secluded spot to have my meal in peace.

Later, when I went looking for her, I was scandalised to find her sniffing at the sweets and *rasmalai* at the dessert counter. Seeing my quizzical look, she explained that one of her friends had told her that folks in Rajasthan used camel's milk, and she wanted to smell the difference. I assured her that no camel was in any way associated with the food, and she looked relieved.

Thankfully, after she was well-fed and watered, she sat down and decided to watch the wedding rituals in enraptured silence. I brought two mishti-*paans* from the *paan*-counter and made sure she stuffed one into her mouth before I sat down next to her for a blissful period of silence. I heaved a sigh of relief. The two *paans* would gift me at least 20 minutes of silence, after which it would be time to leave. Even amidst all the gold glittering on all the ladies around, her silence seemed golden and precious to me.

Mishti Mashi Turns into a Match-maker

Mishti Mashi (MM) was worried as her only daughter, Taniya, was refusing to get married. MM kept badgering her to tie the knot every day, and lately had also developed the uncanny ability to steer any conversation towards marriage.

One day, Taniya forgot to send an attachment in the mail. MM had chided her, "What would you know of attachment? You need to get married to understand love and attachment."

MM had also put an ad in the matrimonial (newspaper) — 'Suitable match required for Bengali, Hindu girl, JNU-educated journalist, 26, fair, slim.'

Thankfully, after visiting Taniya's hostel room one day (which she had not cleaned for three weeks), she had removed the word 'homely' from the ad. She met some prospective grooms thereafter. MM preferred Bengali men, except in cases where a non-Bengali earned a package exceeding 20 lakhs.

Moreover, MM took it upon herself to write Taniya's profile in the matrimonial websites, which explained why the afore-mentioned prospective grooms were shell-shocked when Taniya ordered a beer (according to the website, she was a strict teetotaller) or cursed loudly (she was supposed to be 'shy and docile').

Lately, even my male colleagues (bachelors) had started complaining that MM had befriended them in Facebook and, without even so much as a preamble, regularly attacked them with questions like 'what is the exact time of your birth' or 'what is your annual family income' or the deadliest question of them all 'are you a *Bangaal* or a *Ghoti*?'

Taniya was no longer entrusted to go out alone with these guys after she blew perfectly round smoke rings in the face of her last suitor when he had enquired about her culinary skills.

In her defence, some of these suitors were more bizarre than the COVID guidelines. Moreover, MM's screening of these guys from the websites was hardly foolproof. The last boy that Taniya had met had claimed to be an English professor at a reputed university. After the first phone conversation with Taniya (It had gone something like this: "You are liking Hindi phillums? Let us go to cinema hall and see a phillum tomorrow...", "I am liking shopping too much and I buy only high-cost brands..."), she realized that he was just as much an English Prof as she was an astronaut!

Anyway, this desultory groom-hunting went on and on, becoming more rushed with each passing year.

MM called me desperately one morning. "Hellooo, are you busy tomorrow?"

Now, this was a tricky question. I wanted to tell her that whether I was busy depended on the rest of the information she was about to provide. If she was inviting me out to dinner, I wasn't too busy, but if I had to run errands for her, I was super-busy.

"Come on. It's been ages since we met. We hardly have any family get-togethers nowadays. You must be missing a lot of family time." With her in the picture, I would not say I was 'missing' it.

Anyway, by the time I could come up with a suitable excuse for not meeting her, she had convinced me to accompany her and Taniya for lunch, where we would meet this guy, Navin, and his mother.

She hung up, saying, "I have only two words for you. Thank you"

I also had two words for her: 'GET HELP,' but she hung up before I could tell her.

Navin and his mother came in a black Verna. I was a bit confused to see 'Joy Maa Taaba' written in Bangla on the rear windshield. Was Taaba some mysterious God/cult that we were unaware of? However, closer scrutiny revealed that it was meant to be Maa Taara, and the dot in the word 'Taara' had faded out. After the mystery of the missing dot was solved, I concentrated on the prospective groom.

Navin looked like an overgrown child, with his pudgy frame, round face, thick glasses, and well-oiled hair. He sat down awkwardly, fiddling with his thumbs.

MM whispered to me, "Won't they make a lovely couple? I can already feel the underlying electricity between them."

(Electricity? Even Ghaziabad had more electricity, what with all the power-cuts.)

We ordered soup and sandwiches. I fervently hoped that MM wouldn't ask the waiter to split one soup into three, like she always did. She pointed at the menu and asked the waiter in a fake accent, "*Yeh kya hai*? Man-chaha soup."

"It's Manchow soup", I hissed in her ear while Taniya snorted into her hanky.

We sat there awkwardly while Navin slurped the soup loudly. Taniya glared at him. I knew MM had woken her up early today, and without at least three cups of strong coffee, she would not have adequate emotional strength to deal with loud slurping noises.

A couple with a baby was initially sitting at the table next to ours. Now, the baby was crawling on all fours throughout the restaurant while the mother chased him. The baby went to the wall and started licking it. Navin's mother looked at him and said fondly, "My Navin also used to lick the walls like him when he was little."

I looked at Taniya. She was sitting with a stony expression. Navin's childhood preference for Nerolac instead of Cerelac did not seem to impress her at all.

Not to be outdone, MM pitched in, "My Taniya was the sweetest. She was very shy as a kid. Even now, she's like that. *Arrey baba,* I see the college kids nowadays. *Ufff,* they are all drinking and doing drugs. My Taniya is not like that at all."

(Yeah, we all know that you do not pay her enough pocket money for her to have a drug problem. As far as drinks were concerned, I had seen six glasses of rum'n coke going down her throat faster than a fat kid on a see-saw.)

Navin's mother suddenly steered the conversation: "Navin is very career-oriented, and you, *beta*?"

Navin announced confidently, "I believe in giving *110%* in everything."

I could not resist and muttered, "Thank God you're not a statistician."

Taniya smirked, but Navin just frowned — the poor fellow clearly did not catch the joke.

Trying again, he clarified, "No, I mean, whatever I do, I always give my 100%."

"Well then," I said with a perfectly straight face, "you should never donate blood."

That did it — Taniya and I burst into giggles like schoolgirls, while Navin still looked utterly lost.

MM whispered in my ear, "Enough with the wisecracks."

MM started talking to Navin's mother. "Taniya is so helpful, y'know. She wakes up early daily to help me in the kitchen with the chores."

I nearly choked on my soup while Taniya patted my back loudly. You see, the sudden closure of my pharyngeal walls that contributed to the choking was brought about by a memory. I remembered the one time we went on vacation to Darjeeling, and I woke Taniya up at the crack of dawn to see the sunrise at Tiger Hills. My blood still turned cold at the memory. The moment I woke her up, she shook with rage and grabbed my T-shirt and hissed like a venomous rattlesnake, with bloodshot eyes, "Listen, and listen carefully: no sunrise in the world is beautiful enough to wake me up so early. Do you get it? DON'T EVER FORGET THAT." That was the last time I ever woke someone up. As far as chores were concerned, she had never tidied up her room even once. Her housekeeping style could best be described as 'there appears to have been some struggle.'

MM described her with great admiration — "She's the ideal girl: obedient, soft-spoken, kind, and generous." Then she turned to me with a pointed look and asked, "Don't you agree?"

(I'd agree with you, but then we would both be wrong!)

MM continued with what seemed like a well-rehearsed, premeditated and somewhat irrelevant soliloquy. Excerpts of whatever I remember of this extremely one-sided conversation are as follows:

"Ultimately, I believe, one should accept one's own self, however they are."

(Unless one is a serial killer, and then one should not accept, but try to change, I suppose.)

"Just look around. Everyone has problems, but my Taniya never runs away from her problems."

(Of course, she doesn't run away from her problems; she sits on the sofa, watches television, fiddles with her phone and ignores them just like everyone else.)

"In our lives, it's the right attitude that matters. I know some people who can smile even in a crisis."

(From my experience, the one who smiles in a crisis has found someone to blame!)

After her philosophy had drained out, she turned to Taniya with moist eyes. "My father also loved Taniya very much. I am sure he is looking down on you from Heaven right now."

MM's father (my grandfather) was a very condescending man, and he looked down on us even when he was alive, so that was nothing to write home about.

"What did you say?" MM suddenly asked me.

"Who, me? Nothing." I replied quickly, trying to sound casual.

I must have rolled my eyes out loud! I kept my mouth shut after that, as my mouth usually got me into trouble, and if it wasn't my mouth, it was my facial expressions.

MM asked Taniya, "Okay, *beta,* why don't you two talk while we take a stroll outside?" Saying this, she nudged my elbow. I got the hint and was about to get up when Taniya shoved the small of my back firmly and pushed me down. She obviously did not want to be left alone with this unknown creature.

The mothers left while I sat awkwardly between Taniya and Navin. Nobody spoke a word, and the awkwardness was almost palpable.

I tried to cut through the eerie silence: "Say, Navin, this is hardly the perfect set-up for you to meet Taniya, right? What do you think would be the perfect date?"

He looked skywards and there were deep lines on his forehead as he concentrated like I had asked him some formula in trigonometry, "The perfect date would be 5th February. It's neither too hot nor too cold."

I corrected myself hurriedly. "No, I mean, a perfect date as in the perfect place for you two to meet alone and chit-chat."

Taniya glared at me, and I quickly shut up. She was highly prone to mood swings, but it looked like the chains of one of these swings had just snapped.

Taniya asked Navin curtly, "So, have you met any other girls?"

Navin nodded thoughtfully. "Yes, I did meet one girl once, but my mother didn't like her."

Taniya leaned forward, curious. "Why not?" she asked.

Subtlety was not one of her finer qualities. I could see from his sweaty palms and shifty gaze that he did not want to say.

"Well?" she prompted.

"Well," he gulped. "She told me she had a boyfriend before and had almost got engaged to him."

"So?" Taniya and I chorused.

Navin stuttered, "Well, my m-mother didn't think th-that she was all that good. I mean, a b-boyfriend and all."

I didn't really understand the reason for his dull-wittedness, but I admired his total commitment to it.

Taniya crossed her arms and fixed Navin with a determined glare. "Okay, look here, Navin. First of all."

Now, from years of experience, I knew this was the moment to panic. Whenever Taniya began a sentence with *"First of all,"* it was a clear warning to drop everything and run for cover. Those ominous words always meant she had done her homework — complete with research, pie charts, pivot tables, and enough evidence to prove her point and completely annihilate her opponent.

Navin, however, was unaware of these facts. He just sat there stupidly, basking in his stupidity or whatever, while Taniya lashed out at him savagely. All the thoughts in her head went for a quick stroll through her mouth, and that is rarely a good thing. Her diatribe abated after three minutes. By then, Navin looked like he had jumped on a bicycle only to discover the absence of its seat.

Taniya stormed off to the ladies' room to cool off, while I stood there sheepishly, facing Navin.

I opened my mouth, trying to think of something intelligent to say. "Well, er..."

Navin looked at me expectantly. "Yes?"

"Umm, I'd love to stand here and talk to you," I said, backing away slowly, "but I'm not going to."

And with that, I hurried after Taniya.

We found MM hovering near the washroom, anxiously waiting.

"Well? How did it go? What do you feel?" she asked the moment she saw us.

(Is 'ugh' an emotion? This is because that's exactly what I felt.)

I wanted to tell her the whole experience reminded me of the time she convinced Taniya to buy organic vegetables for dinner — and then ordered pizza instead.

A moment later, Taniya emerged from the nearby loo, her face giving absolutely nothing away — classic poker-face mode.

"Well," she said casually, "Navin didn't like me all that much…" She shrugged as if it were no big deal.

MM looked completely dumbfounded. "But why not?"

"They're looking for a super-rich girl and a handsome dowry," Taniya replied matter-of-factly. "So, yeah, I guess that's it."

"WHAT! Is he mad?" MM sputtered.

"My guess is he just hasn't been diagnosed yet," I muttered.

To cut a long story short, that was the last that we saw or heard of Navin. The fruitless search for Taniya's groom still continued, but I made sure I was never dragged into it again.

Adventures with Anuj and Anwesha

First Impression

I was in my fourth year of college. The semester exams were over, and Durga Puja was just around the corner. My friend/batchmate Anwesha had invited some of us to her place on Ashtami, as Durga Puja was celebrated with much gusto in her ancestral house.

Now, Anwesha was dating a Punjabi guy, Anuj Verma, from Chandigarh, who was also my batchmate. Her plan was to invite him along with us and introduce him to her parents. Belonging to a conservative family, she knew her parents would disapprove of him, and so she solicited my help. I was the most sought-after ally for these offbeat endeavours, thanks to my subtle and scheming intellect. I agreed readily, of course, partly because I am very generous by nature, but mostly because she had done all the sketches in my Anatomy Practicals and I would need her involvement in the forthcoming Surgery Practicals as well.

After the Ashtami rituals were over and we were stuffed up to our larynges with the delicious bhog and luchis, we all sat down together in her sprawling living room. Anwesha's father loved singing, and she had warned us that he would flood us with a torrent of Rabindra Sangeet as soon as lunch was over. Sure enough, Uncle occupied centre-stage in the living room, armed and dangerous with the ominous harmonium. We sat meekly around him in a semi-circle, waiting to be engulfed by the dulcet tunes!

He asked us, more out of courtesy than actual curiosity, *"Tomra keu gaan koro? Ekta gaan gao na."* (Do any of y'all sing? Do sing a song then.)

We all shook our heads politely, but to my utter bewilderment, Anuj seemed all gung-ho about it and volunteered readily.

"Thank you, *paaji.*" he said and stood up.

I was sitting right next to Uncle, and he looked at me quizzically and whispered, *"Ki bollo? Amake paaji bollo?"* (Did he call me *paaji*? The word *'Paaji'* means 'mischievous' in Bengali).

I explained to him that the word *'paaji'* is used to address someone older in Punjabi.

Now, I had only heard Anuj sing once, at our college fest. He had sung a new-age song titled *'Tan tana tan tantan taara'*. I fervently hoped that he would not dish out that song because it was definitely too 'avant-garde' for the present gathering. Anyone who had the misfortune of hearing him sing in the fest, followed by his frenzied dancing, would vouch for the fact that singing was definitely not one of his finer talents and not the first trait to demonstrate if he wanted to impress any prospective in-laws, bosses and so on. I mean, everyone has a right to be stupid, but it looked like he was abusing the privilege.

Suddenly, without any warning, Anuj cleared his throat noisily and burst out into a Bengali song.

"Janina ki gaibo ami..." he sang. (Don't know what I will sing...)

Uncle interrupted him, *"Gao na, je kono gaan gao. Lojja peo na."* (Sing any song, don't feel shy.)

I whispered to Uncle that he was already in the process of singing, and the song was, unfortunately, titled *"Janina ki gaibo ami"* from a movie called Nater Guru. Obviously, the lack of a mellifluous voice had rendered the melody rather flat. However, before I could explain further, the damage was already done. Anuj blushed brighter than a beetroot and kept on opening and shutting his mouth like a goldfish, his confidence deflating faster than a punctured balloon. He sat down shortly and busied himself looking attentively at his fingernails.

Thereafter, Uncle regaled us with a series of Rabindra Sangeet, and we listened quietly, clapping loudly at intervals. After the pandemonium à la harmonium was over, we scattered here and there. I kept my eye on Anuj to ensure that there would be no more mishaps. As far as impressing Anwesha's parents was concerned, it looked like he had hit rock-bottom. Little did I know that the worst was yet to come; it seemed that his 'rock-bottom' had a basement.

After some time, Anwesha's mother found us and, looking at Anuj, asked him amicably, *"Toom aaj paanjaabi pehnaa? Bahoot aachcha, haamko paanjabi bahoot acchcha laagta hai."* (A kurta is often called 'paanjabi' in Bengali. Her words maybe loosely be translated as "You wore a paanjabi? Very nice, I like it very much.")

Now, Anuj's vocabulary in Bengali was pretty much in the nascent stage, but he seemed elated at her words and replied, grinning from ear to ear, *"Aapko Punjabi log acche lagte hai, Aunty? Humko bhi bongs bahut pasand hai."*

Bewildered, Aunty stuttered, *"Arre naa… maney... eeye...kurta ko haamlog banglaye panjaabi bolta hai."*

Saying this, she scurried away upstairs on the pretext of attending to guests.

Anuj turned to me, his face scarlet and a vein popping in his forehead. For some reason, whatever Aunty had said really got his goat.

"Kya boli woh?" he hissed at me. *"Kutta ko Bangaali log 'Punjabi' bolta hai? Kutta hoga unka."*

I tried in vain to stop his tirade, but he lashed out with a string of colourful words, most of which I cannot reproduce here because some of my teachers are also reading this story. Although I marvelled at his enriched vocabulary, I quickly mollified him after his diatribe had abated somewhat. He still looked at me suspiciously, clenching his fists. His Punjabi blood was boiling, no doubt, and the *'sher da puttar'* was rearing his head inside him, I suppose. I had to think on my feet fast.

After his blood had cooled down to room temperature or thereabouts, I took him to a corner and explained a master plan that I had chalked out. My plan was simple. He was to go to Aunty, upstairs, and talk to her. I knew Aunty was an ardent Tagore fan, so I had told Anuj to tell her that she reminded him of Labanya, the heroine in Tagore's novel, *Shesher Kobita*. For those of my readers who are dumbfounded and have not quite captured the essence of this conniving ploy, allow me to explain.

Aunty happened to be a voracious reader of Tagore's work, and she was also an independent-minded woman. In other words, she listened to her husband and took his advice about as frequently as a pigeon used a bicycle. This fact had been affirmed by none other than her own offspring, viz. Anwesha. Hence, the comparison to Labanya, Tagore's heroine, seemed like a fitting tribute to her, for anyone who desired to be in her good books. I strongly advocated for Anuj to use the adjectives 'confident' and 'intelligent' while describing Aunty, as I did not rely too much on his own vocabulary.

Being intuitive since childhood, I presumed that Aunty would be suitably impressed that Anuj, being a Punjabi, had read *Shesher Kobita* and would be suitably thrilled that he had compared her to Labanya. Come on, it's common knowledge that every woman who has read the novel harbours a secret dream to be Labanya. After apprising him of the finer nuances of the plot, I was confident that the scheme seemed foolproof from all angles.

I waited with bated breath and glanced at my watch, waiting for Anuj to return. He returned exactly after 15 minutes, beaming like a little girl who had discovered a secret stash of candies. He told me that my plan had worked wonders; Aunty was gushing, telling everyone within earshot that she had been compared with Labanya.

I heaved a sigh of relief, feeling that my work here was done. It would be safe to say that I basked in the glory of my brilliantly successful plan. I went to Aunty to take her leave. After the brainstorming that day, I was exhausted and badly needed a siesta to rejuvenate the grey cells.

Aunty whispered in my ear while I was leaving, *"Chheleta khub bhalo re, toke khub khushi rakhbe. Biyete amader oboshhoyi daakbi."* (The guy is really nice; he will keep you very happy. Do invite us to your wedding.)

Aghast, I vehemently denied the allegations and tried to explain that there was absolutely no chemistry or biology between me and Anuj. However, she just laughed merrily and pushed me away, saying, *"Tui ki bhabli? Tora ek konaye phish-phish korchilish, amra keu dekhini? Amar emni emni chul pakeni re, shob bujhi...ha ha ha."* ("Did you think we didn't see you whispering together in the corner? It's not for nothing that my hair has greyed, I notice everything...ha ha ha.")

My flailing arms and flummoxed expression only drew more guffaws from the other aunties. Anuj beamed at everyone benevolently, looking absolutely calm amidst the chaos, not because he had attained 'inner peace' but probably because he had not completely understood the situation. Before I could clarify anything further, Aunty had disappeared into a sea of other aunties.

I returned home in a cab with Anuj, with a heavy stomach and a heavier heart. Anuj sang a Rabindra Sangeet, tunelessly, all the way, indulging in his newfound penchant for this particular genre and doing grave injustice to it, in the process.

The Staged Performance

Every year on Rabindra Jayanti (the birthday of Rabindranath Tagore), our college hosts a program featuring Tagore's songs and plays. My best friend and batchmate, Anwesha, was dating Anuj, a regular Punjabi guy (also our batchmate). Many of you may have read my earlier story about Anuj's failed attempt at impressing Anwesha's parents.

On the day of Rabindra Jayanti, Anwesha's parents decided to attend our college program as their darling daughter would be performing in one of Tagore's famous plays. Anwesha was adamant that Anuj must try his best to win over her parents that day and had made me grudgingly participate in this humongous endeavour. If you had followed my last memoir with proper care, you would agree that this was a seemingly impossible enterprise. Anyway, I couldn't let Anwesha, my bestie, down (also, she gave me her notes before every exam).

The day of Rabindra Jayanti was bright and clear with a promising azure sky. We were all seated in our sprawling sports ground, and our Professors were on stage. The program started with the quintessential 'Welcome note' followed by a speech on Tagore's early life.

Anwesha sat between her parents, whereas I sat next to her father, and Anuj sat next to me.

Our plan was simple: Anuj should speak intelligently to Uncle (Anwesha's father) and try to get into his good books.

We had tutored him about Tagore's works, and all he had to do was sing praises about the bearded bard, which was sure to soften Anwesha's parents, given that they were both ardent fans of Tagore. We could not think of a better plan for how Anuj could impress them. Anuj's hobbies included laughing hard at his own jokes and sleeping in class, not exactly the kind of thing his parents would approve of.

We sat silently for a few minutes. Both Uncle and Aunty were following the program with rapt attention.

I whispered to Anuj, "Say something to Uncle, *na*."

"I don't want to be too pushy, *yaar*", he whispered to me, "You start talking first."

I said irritably, "*Arrey*, Anuj, why play so hard to get when you're already so hard to like?"

Anuj said, "What?"

I replied, "Nothing, forget it."

When I described Anuj earlier as a regular guy, I may have been exaggerating slightly. He was a little slow on the uptake.

I initiated some small talk with Uncle, and he started reminiscing about his school days when he would play all the lead roles in his school plays. He also told me that he had dabbled in theatre and had shared the stage with a Tollywood actress, which I had missed because I was in the cradle at the time. Apparently, Aunty had also performed in a few plays, wowing the audience with her espieglerie and dialogue delivery! He had gotten to the point where he told me that their reputation as talented actors had been established amongst the cognoscenti, when suddenly Anuj butted in, "Uncle, I also have a small role in the next play. I am going to be a beggar."

Uncle murmured something under his breath, which I could not hear exactly, but it sounded a lot like: "If you didn't have a rich dad, you would have been a beggar much earlier."

Anuj said, "Sorry, Uncle, I didn't catch what you said."

Uncle shrugged nonchalantly and said, "Oh, nothing."

I looked at Uncle, and 'grouchy' was the word that came to mind. In fact, if I had to cast him in a role right then, I would prefer a Russian drama where he would announce soberly that grandpa had hanged himself in the backyard. That was how grouchy he had sounded.

I felt sorry for Anuj. I wanted to tell him that nothing in life is more brutally honest than children, tight-fitted clothes and the parents of the girl you like, but it seemed an inopportune moment to do so.

Suddenly, the anchor on stage yelled into the mic, "For the first time ever, we have here on stage a Punjabi student who will sing a Rabindra Sangeet. Please welcome on stage Anuj Vermaaaa."

Anuj got up from his seat and sauntered confidently onto the stage. I looked at Anwesha, shell-shocked. This was not part of the plan.

Anuj had decided to surprise (shock) us. I remembered the fiasco last time when Anuj had decided to sing a Bengali song during Durga Puja. I murmured under my breath, "Dear déjà vu, I don't want to go through that again."

I recalled our last picnic when Anuj was drunk. He had hollered at the top of his voice, *"Ho gayi tere balle balle, ho jayegi balle balle."* throughout the bus journey back home. We had all requested him to stop singing with folded hands, but he had kept on shouting something that sounded like: *"ha-hak-chiki-*

nak-chikinak chikinak." till all our ears were ringing. To make matters worse, he had also decided to perform bhangra on the moving bus and had urged everyone to dance, but no one had volunteered to join in his merry mélange. However, he had continued dancing like an untamed monkey, unfettered, till the last bus stop.

However, it looked like Anuj did not need alcohol to make bad decisions this time. I looked at Anwesha, who was staring at him, aghast and quivering like a blanc-mange! Generally, the things that you are scared about the most in your imagination are not as scary in real life. However, this was not the case with Anuj's singing that day.

He croaked into the mic, *"Jodi tor daak shune keu naa ashey…tobe ekla cholo re."* I don't mind admitting that I winced. I was wrong to think that Anuj was a poor decision-maker… he wasn't. He was just fundamentally unsound.

After the first few seconds, many people got up from their seats, preferring to leave him *'ekla'* (alone), no doubt. However, the scarce audience couldn't discourage Anuj, who, always a glutton for punishment, continued yelling tunelessly and nodding his head rhythmically at intervals. In fact, he started singing even more loudly, and his vocal cords showed signs of cracking under the strain. His symptoms, I later found out, were attributed to a condition called 'clergyman's throat' which resulted because he had been practising his beastly singing over the past few days and doing grave injustice to his larynx, in the process. He continued the frog-like rendition of the song, and his joie de vivre was only dampened somewhat when Anwesha's parents also got up from their seats and left. No matter how you look at it, his performance was a total washout. The only bit of blue amidst the clouds was the fact that he only sang for 1.5 minutes, as he could not remember the entire song.

People clapped fervently when Anuj had stopped singing (probably because he had stopped). I took a long, hard look at Anuj when he was getting off the stage, looking smug and waving at everyone. His life seemed to be running according to Murphy's Law: 'If anything can go wrong, it will… ' (Okay, I'm not 100% sure which law it is.)

Anuj whispered to me, "Was it good?"

By 'it' he meant the cacophony of sounds which he thought was a song. The words which would best describe 'it' accurately were: 'perfectly foul'. However, I exercised tact and muttered under my breath: "Let's put it this way — you were the human equivalent of a participation award."

"What's that?" Anuj asked.

I said, "Nothing."

Even a sloth would be faster than him at comprehending stuff. I looked at him, trying to figure out why Anwesha liked him in the first place. He was one of those guys whom one could never fall in love with at first sight, and the chances of loving him after a long acquaintance also seemed pretty negligible.

While I was thus musing and shaking my head in pity about Anuj slipping over life's banana skins, he started talking again, "*Accha,* I have a plan."

I said, "Listen, Anuj, I have a complete grasp on the fact that you are the king of bad decisions. You don't have to try so hard to prove it."

Anuj started, "Come on, *yaa…*"

Anuj was cut short by Uncle and Aunty, who had just returned to their seats with cold drinks and chips. Aunty opened a big tiffin box filled with onion pakodas (piyajis) she had cooked and brought from home, and offered them to us.

Now, Anwesha had told Anuj several times that her mother loved it whenever someone praised her culinary skills, so Anuj grabbed this opportunity without any hesitation. Although he was not very original in the praise he showered on Aunty, it looked like he had watched too many episodes of MasterChef Australia.

After taking a bite of one piyaji, Anuj chirped, "Oh, the pakodas are simply delightful, Aunty. They're so crisp on the outside and soft on the inside. The tangy flavours of the rich Indian spices are just oozing into my mouth. They've got such a lovely rustic aftertaste. It's like an explosion, an explo-o-osion of rich flavours and delicate textures. It's like a symphony in my mouth, a symphony of..."

I had to stop him. I elbowed him hard on his ribs, and he nearly choked.

Uncle whispered to me, "Is he on drugs?"

I whispered back, "Come on, Uncle, you and I both know that medical colleges don't pay enough stipend for any of us to have a drug problem."

Uncle glared at me, but I paid no heed to him and continued munching on the piyajis, which passed over my pharynx with a goodish deal of vim and je-ne-sais-quoi. I golfed around seven of them before Anuj interrupted me again.

"Hey, how did you like me praising Aunty? My English was good, *na*?"

I said, "Yes, you have not been yourself lately; we have all noticed the improvement."

Anuj said, "I think I will inspire many."

I wanted to tell him that he was, indeed, inspiring my inner serial killer.

I looked up at the sky and asked God, "Dear God, when I asked you earlier...could the day get any worse? It was merely a hypothetical question and not a challenge."

I looked at Uncle. He seemed least interested in Anuj and had immersed his whole being in the piyajis only to resurface every 5 minutes or so for a longish, irritatingly audible slurp of tea. When I had asked Anwesha about her father, she had assured me, "Oh, he is a lamb…so amicable and lovable." However, on close scrutiny, I found no lamb-like qualities in him, and even our college Principal seemed more amicable than he.

I started talking to him, "How was your journey, Uncle? Hope you had no problem coming here?"

Sipping another ounce of the Oolong, he looked up at me slowly and said, "*Arrey*, you know what happened? A student on a bike nearly collided with my car. These college kids drive so recklessly, I tell you."

Anuj said, "Yes, Uncle, I totally agree. In fact, accidents are usually man-made. I'm sure 90% of all people are caused by accidents.

I choked on the piyajis and said, "You mean...90% of all accidents are caused by people?"

Anuj said, "Ah, yes, yes. That's what I meant."

Anuj looked mortified. He had blushed crimson, with his red earlobes and cheeks; he looked like an explosion of tomato ketchup over a sky at sunrise.

I did not know what to say; the ambience was sombre. Aunty looked at Uncle with a goodish deal of solemnity while he slurped gravely at his cup of tea. It was one of those moments which authors describe as time standing still. I felt bad for Anuj and thanked God that it was him, and not me, who would have these two as future in-laws! Anyone would shrink from the prospect of being decanted into a household of such silent and moody tea-sippers.

After a minute, Uncle looked into his teacup and said, hesitantly, *"Yeh chaa mein ek chul hain."* (There's a strand of hair in my tea.)

Anuj asked me, *"Kya boley who? Chai peeke woh chull hai?"* (What did he say? He is 'high' after drinking tea?)

Uncle said, *"Kudi takar chaa...Tar moddhey abar chul."*

(The tea is worth Rs. 20, but even then, there's a hair in it!)

Anuj hissed at me, *"Kya bol raha hai Uncle! Kaunsi kudi chull hai? Samajh mein nahi aa raha hai."* (What is Uncle saying? Which girl is 'high'? I can't understand anything.)

Uncle, calling Anuj, said, *"Arrey Anuj beta...woh chai-wala dada ko bulao."* (*Arrey* Anuj, call that tea-seller.)

Anuj said, *"Arrey paaji...Aap usko 'dada' kyon bol rahe ho? Itna young sa toh banda hai."* (Why are you calling him grandfather? He is such a young guy.)

Uncle, who was visibly cringing at being called 'paaji,' said, *"Uff kotha bola tao chaap...Ki chaap re baba."* (It is so difficult to talk to him.)

Anuj heaved a sigh of relief and said, *"Oh, Chaap chahiye aapko? Chaap idhar milta hai Uncle — Chicken aur mutton chaap...dono hi milta hai... Lekin abhi canteen khula nahi hai."* (Both chicken and mutton chaap are available here.)

Aunty suddenly sprang up from her seat and cried out, *"Arrey, ek bolta hai mere chair ke neeche ... Ota ke tarao, tarao."* (There's a wasp under my chair, please get rid of it.)

Anuj said, *"Aapka chair bolta hain?"* (Your chair speaks?). Then, turning to me, he whispered, *"Aunty kya bol rahi hai yaar?"*

I pitied poor Anuj. It was like his life was a series of embarrassing moments punctuated by some poor translation. I looked at him. His eyes were downcast, and he looked like a castaway who had abandoned all hope. His voice, when he spoke, was like a voice from the grave.

"Do something, *na*." he urged me.

I mused for a bit and wondered when the last time that I had been so rattled. Then I had a eureka moment. I whispered my plan to Anuj and told him, "You have to do this."

Hearing my plan, Anuj said, "You're pulling my leg."

"Nothing would induce me to pull your ghastly leg," I said.

Anuj finally agreed, and after giving me a weak smile, the kind that soldiers give before going to fight in the border area, he got up from his seat and went on stage. Snatching the mic from the anchor, he bellowed, "Friends, we have all paid our tribute to the great Tagore, but we have here, amidst us, two of the greatest fans of Tagore. Both of them love Rabindra Sangeet, and I request them to please come on stage and sing a duet for us before we conclude today's program.

"Ladies and gentlemen, please give it up for…Mr Joy Bhattacharya and Mrs Rima Bhattacharya…Proud parents of Anwesha."

Anwesha and I stood up, clapping hard while Aunty blushed and looked at me. Uncle looked too pleased for words. I knew he was thrilled as he never missed an opportunity to unleash the harmonium on us and regale us with Rabindra Sangeet whenever we had paid Anwesha a visit.

They went up to the stage gingerly and sang a duet. Their performance was met with much applause, cheering, and hooting (we had urged all our friends to continue clapping for at least 2 minutes flat).

Aunty came back to her seat and, adjusting her silk saree, exclaimed, *"ei Anuj ta na, sotti baba, amar eto lojja korchilo."* (This Anuj is too much; I was feeling so shy.)

However, she was grinning from ear to ear. Uncle seemed elated, *"Arrey, beta,* you could've told us earlier, we would've rehearsed and come *na.*"

Anuj chirped, *"Uncle, it was fatafati."* He knew only three words in Bangla. One of them was 'fatafati', and the other two cannot be reproduced here.

Uncle said with a smile on his face, *"Heh heh, come here, beta."*

Anuj said shyly, "Who? Me?" He seemed startled. Probably, the poor fellow was not accustomed to such a gluttonous appetite for his own company.

Uncle asked, "Music is in our souls, beta. By the way, where are you from?"

Anuj replied, "I am from Chandigarh, Uncle."

Uncle said, "Oh, that's too far."

I whispered, "Relax, Uncle, he's not inviting you home."

Uncle, not being able to understand what I said, asked, "What?"

"Nothing." I replied.

Anwesha glared at me and chided me for my persiflage while Anuj was simply glowing. I just hoped he would not break out in bhangra soon.

I looked at them both and smiled. My good deed for the day was done. I staggered away from this family reunion in search of solitude or repose, or preferably, both. I made my way to my hostel room, where a girl, without encumbrances in the form of uncles and aunts, might be able to spend a restful day or two.

The Mystery of the Silver Swan

This happened during my medical college days. My best friend Anwesha's parents were going on a vacation to Vizag, but Anwesha could not go because of our semester exams. So, her parents came to meet her and decided to spend the night in our hostel's guest room.

Now, Anwesha was dating a Punjabi guy named Anuj (our batchmate), and his last few attempts to impress her parents had proved futile. We decided that he should give it another go.

After much thought, we formulated a master plan. It appeared to be foolproof. Anwesha's father always carried a small silver swan with him, calling it a good luck charm! He even kept it on the bedside table while sleeping. My plan was simple. We convinced Paanchu (the ward boy who worked at the hostel and ran errands for us) to help us by bribing him with mutton biryani.

Paanchu was to stealthily go into the guest room at night, while both Aunty and Uncle would be fast asleep and nick the silver swan. Then, he was to surreptitiously creep out of the room and meet us outside. I would then shout *"chor... chor...,"* waking everyone up. Uncle would wake up and, upon realising that his silver swan was missing, come out of the room. We would then tell him that we had seen a robber running away with his silver swan. Anuj had caught him and snatched the swan from him, but couldn't catch the robber, as he had sprinted.

The plan was ready. Anuj and I waited patiently outside the guest room after dinner. Anuj was looking both scared and excited.

He said dramatically, "Wish I could go and steal the swan myself, but it's better Paanchu does it."

I challenged him immediately, "Why? You can do it. Don't be a coward."

Anuj protested and said, "Hey, I'm not a coward. My friends call me 'sher da puttar'."

I assured him, "I'm not calling you totally spineless; I just think you have no more backbone than a jellyfish."

Anuj did not appreciate the sarcasm and said, "Very funny. This time, I'm sure Aunty and Uncle will like me."

I said, with a look of disappointment, "Difficult, seeing that you have the charisma of a wet rag and the appearance of a burly butler."

He stared at me and asked, "Don't you like anything about me? Anything that I do?"

I replied, "I like that thing when you don't call me for weeks… adorable."

Offended, he declared, "Okay, I'm not talking to you again."

I said joyfully, "You're giving me the silent treatment? Yesss, finally!"

Anuj said, "I feel insulted."

I told him, "If I said anything to offend you, it was purely intentional."

He complained, "Doctors should be helpful, you are not helping."

I assured him, "Okay, okay, we'll make you the hero of this story. If doctors can make penicillin out of mouldy bread, then we can make something out of you, too."

He said cheerfully, "And you can help me write some poetry, for Anwesha."

I remarked, "No, every poet is a fool, but every fool can't be a poet."

Anuj said angrily, "Shut up, I am also learning acting, to act in the college play, because she loves theatre."

I suggested, "You can play the role of the corpse."

He said with a look of disgust: "*Ufff.*"

I had to help him. Firstly, Anwesha was my best friend, and secondly, Anuj was not really a bad guy. He was just like a case of herpes (always inconvenient and embarrassing, not a real threat, though… but just won't go away). He may look like an idiot and talk like an idiot, but don't let that fool you; he really is an idiot. Anyway, we continued bantering for some more time. Exactly at 1:30am, as planned, Paanchu crept into the guest room. We waited patiently outside for Paanchu to emerge, but he didn't. Suddenly, a sharp cry emanated from the guest room, piercing the stillness of the night.

We rushed into the room and saw that Uncle and Aunty were standing shell-shocked while Paanchu was lying on the floor, writhing in pain.

The silver swan was lying on the floor. The neck of the swan had opened, and at least half a dozen cigarettes (presumably from inside the swan) lay scattered on the floor.

Uncle uttered a coarse expletive which I would not have believed he would have known. It just shows that one can bury oneself in Tagore's works, in Anandabazar Patrika, and even play the harmonium, yet still acquire a colourful vocabulary. Perhaps it can be attributed to his early-morning visits to the local fish market. Otherwise, it would be extremely difficult to explain the torrent of words that escaped him shortly, like bats fluttering out of a barn.

Uncle looked at Paanchu, "Who are you? What are you doing in this room?"

I said, "It is Paanchu, the ward-boy, uncle. He often walks in his sleep."

Uncle disagreed with me and said, "Nobody sleepwalks like this."

I tried to explain the science of sleepwalking like a governess explaining rudimentary arithmetic to an intellectually-challenged child.

Uncle said, "No, no, I actually trod on him. He was nestling on the floor near my bed. Like a snake, uninvited, encroaching on my personal space. You ask him. He was oozing all over the floor like oil."

I envisaged the scene and cringed. I could picture it only too clearly. Paanchu must have been crawling, and while he aimed for the silver swan, uncle's number 10-sized foot must have descended upon something squashy (Paanchu had later revealed to us that it was some sensitive part of his anatomy), and Paanchu had yelped in pain.

Having told Aunty that he had stopped smoking years ago, Uncle must have waited for her to drift off to sleep and then sneaked outside for a smoke.

All this while, Aunty was looking aghast at the cigarettes. Suddenly, she exploded into a non-stop diatribe: *"E ki? Tumi cigarette khao? Tumi na bolechhile j cigarette chhere diechho?"* (You still smoke? Didn't you tell me that you had left smoking?)

She looked livid. Her face, resembling a crushed strawberry, now deepened in colour and resembled a beetroot at its ripest. She lashed out at him and not only dissected his penchant for nicotine, but gave some crisp remarks about his general physique, lack of a disciplined lifestyle and in general, his lackadaisical approach to everything in life. However, she did not stop there. She went on to criticise his family tree, his schooling, his friends, his habit of slurping tea loudly, his lack of punctuality, his sense of dress, his snoring, etc. By the end of the tirade, he was reduced to the lowest ranks of human beings possible… perhaps he fared slightly better than a serial killer on the loose (but only marginally).

I looked at Uncle. He had always looked like an overgrown, angry cat. Now, he looked like one who had been refused a slice of fish. Aunty glared at Uncle. Uncle glared at Paanchu.

There was a pause. During this pause, Anuj stood up from the chair and drew himself to his full height. Then, noticing that nobody was looking at him, he sat down again.

I whispered, "Anuj, say something."

Anuj said, "*Achha*, Uncle. You snore. I also snore."

We stared speechless at him. It would not be too far off the mark to state here that Anuj had all the sensitivity of a blunt axe.

Anuj said, "I know a joke about snoring, Uncle. A wife had brought her husband to the doctor for snoring, and the doctor wrote in his prescription: 'It was his adenoids that adenoid her.'"

Nobody spoke.

Anuj tried to explain, "His adenoids 'ad annoyed her."

He laughed nervously. It was a solo performance; nothing under the prevailing circumstances convinced anybody to turn it into a duet.

Anuj looked crestfallen. He resembled a child who was talking excitedly about seeing a cannibal, only to have someone tell him that the cannibal was not a cannibal at all but a local, famous vegetarian!

There was yet another pregnant pause. I massaged the forehead. (Mine, of course).

I said, "It's quite a hot night, isn't it?"

Anuj agreed, "Quite hot."

Uncle said, "Very humid too."

Aunty also joined her, saying, "Horrible weather"

Paanchu interjected suddenly, "*Bicchiri gorom.*" (Terrible heat)

That seemed to wrap up the weather bulletin for the day. Once again, an eerie silence enveloped us. I realised that it was no longer within the sphere of realistic expectations to contain the conversation about neutral topics like the weather.

I said, "You remember Anuj, Uncle. He is our friend from Chandigarh."

Uncle nodded, "Yes. Is he Punjabi?"

I replied, "To the core."

Uncle asked, "Isn't he the one for whom Anwesha drew those Anatomy sketches in the practical book?"

I replied, "Of course not, Uncle. Anuj does his own sketches…every work of his is the result of the most strenuous and unremitting efforts on his part."

I was lying, of course. The truth is, anyone could draw better than Anuj (with their left hand).

Anuj whispered to me, "*Ab kya hoga*? What do I say?"

I whispered back, "*Arrey, sab theek ho jayega*... one cannot make an omelette without breaking some eggs."

"Omelette *khabe?*" chimed in Paanchu, the eavesdropping bugger.

Uncle asked, "Omelette?"

He looked at Aunty.

There was another pause that was punctuated by Aunty, who was breathing like an asthma patient.

I asked, "Aunty, would you like some coffee?"

If there was ever a woman who needed a caffeine-induced resurrection, it was she.

Aunty said, "Okay, thanks."

I said, with a smile on my face, "Don't mention it."

Aunty said, "What's the point of saying don't mention it when I have already mentioned it."

I avoided Mrs. Snarky.

I said, "Hey, I have some Belgian chocolates... would anyone like some?"

Anuj replied, "I would."

I said with a stern look, "Sorry, I can't give it to you."

Anuj asked angrily, "Then why did you mention it?"

I replied, "You see, a great deal of pleasure lies in denying it to others."

Paanchu returned soon with steaming hot cups of coffee. Uncle looked at him suspiciously and accepted the coffee. His eyes still had the look of cautious reserve that you will find frequently in pet dogs, when offered a juicy bone by a stranger (about whose credentials they are not fully convinced).

Anuj said, "Uncle, I will tell you a joke about a dog, a cat and a monkey."

I hissed at him under my breath, "Come on, Anuj, this is no time to chew the fat about the animal kingdom. And we don't want to hear a joke; we're already looking at you."

Anuj hissed at me, "I'm a joke, huh? I'm an idiot?"

I replied, "I'm just saying that you have your entire life to be an idiot, why not take today off?"

We ate the omelettes silently and sipped on the coffee.

Time was running out. I had to think on my feet. Firstly, we had to pacify Aunty. My experience told me that on these occasions, innocence pays no dividends, even if the intentions are as pure as the driven snow, or even purer. Playing innocent can only help you so far. Only a subtle and scheming intellect can save you, without a stain on your character.

I closed my eyes in concentration, and when I opened them, I saw daylight. Well, not literally, of course, because it was still the middle of the night, but a fairly goodish idea dawned upon me.

I told Anuj to give me the pearl earrings that he had bought to gift to Anwesha. I silently handed them over to Aunty, saying, "Aunty, uncle had bought these earrings for you and had given them to me for safe-keeping."

Uncle looked flabbergasted. Then the look of realisation dawned in his eyes and he stuttered, "Ye-yes...Your birthday is next month...So, I went to the store."

Aunty said angrily, "Don't talk to me."

Uncle said, "And I said to myself."

Aunty said, "But not to me."

Uncle said, "Okay, then once again, I will be dumb."

Aunty said, "And you have been so, from a child."

Uncle tried to convince her, "Okay, I thought you would like it."

Aunty looked at uncle's crestfallen face and seemed a little mollified. She took the earrings and said, "Yes, they're beautiful. It's a good choice."

Uncle said boastfully, "Oh yes, they are real Hyderabadi pearls, you won't get such pearls everywhere."

It is strange how one always yields to the fatal temptation to boast. It undoes the best of us.

They spoke amongst themselves, while I whispered to Anuj, "See, you have to impress Aunty like this: Pitch it strong and let the golden phrases come out of you like honey. Eloquence beyond the ordinary would be of the essence, understand? Now that she's happy with the earrings, you have to do something."

Anuj asked, "Okay, but what do I do?"

I replied, "Remember what Shakespeare wrote? 'There is a tide in the affairs of men, which, taken at the flood, leads on to fortune. Omitted, all the voyage of their life is bound in shallows and in miseries.'"

Anuj asked, clueless, "Floods? Shall I tell them when I nearly drowned in a flood near my grandfather's place?"

It was just scary to know that people like him would be graduating from my college. I could've sworn I was dealing with an adult, but I guess I was mistaken.

I said angrily, "I'm glad you are not letting education get in the way of your stupidity. Don't talk of any floods, unless you were saving an orphaned child."

Anuj said, "Yes, I could say I was taking an orphaned child through the floods. That would make me a hero."

I told him, "You know who the real heroes are? The people who tolerate you on a daily basis. And where exactly were you taking this child to?"

Anuj replied, "To her parents."

I said with a look of disgust, *"Bhai, tu rehne de,* please."

Anuj asked, *"Kyu? Kya hua?* You don't like real-life heroes...You only like those rich silver-screen heroes, roaming around shirtless on some yacht."

I said, "And yet, here you are—shirtless, without a yacht, and not very useful either."

Anuj complained, "Come on, are you saying I am completely useless in life?"

I said, "Oh no, you can be useful, as an organ donor. I'm just saying that you're impossible to be under-estimated."

Anuj said angrily, "You don't have to help me if you hate me."

I said, "I don't hate you, I'm just not very excited about your existence. Okay, I'm sorry."

Anuj complained, "You don't sound apologetic at all."

I said, "I'm sorry if my forced apology sounds insincere, I'll try to make it sound more convincing next time."

Our incessant argument was interrupted by a wayward cat who had entered the room, and we busied ourselves chasing it away. We then returned to our respective rooms and finally called it a day.

The Joke's on Me
(Anecdotes from My Life)

The Mystery of the Bleeding Potatoes

I was around 12 years old then. We used to live in a joint family, with my cousins and grandparents (a total of 11 members). I remember we were always in search of a good cook. My mother used to tell me that my grandparents were too fussy and no cook could last for more than a year, thanks to their incessant demands. Apparently, even the most palatable of dishes were dismissed with a disapproving *"Khub ekta bhalo hoyni."* (Not good enough.) It was obvious (according to my mom) that, after hours of slogging in the hot kitchen, any self-respecting cook would be silently plotting a murder if their entrée were met with a disapproving look and the question, *"Eta ki khawa jaye?"* from our self-proclaimed family connoisseurs.

(My grandmother later told me that it was my parents who were the fussy ones, so I am not completely certain of the facts, but let us not digress.)

Moyna di was our new cook. The last two cooks had fled without any explanation! To everyone's surprise, Moyna di's cooking did not earn the usual snide remarks and impassive faces but was relished with much gusto, finger-licking and second helpings! It was hardly a surprise, then, that she was revered like a Pope and pampered like a newlywed bride with cotton sarees, toys for her kids and occasional packets of sweets!

Now, I was quite a prankster in my childhood, but most of the adults in the family always turned a blind eye to my pranks, thanks to the fact that I was the class topper (Bengalis and their weakness for academics)! Unfortunately, my cousins loathed me for this exact reason! My baby-like cherubic face and innocent eyes also ensured that I was never too harshly reprimanded for my transgressions! Several times, my cousins got into trouble for some prank I had pulled off or got admonished due to some sarcastic repartee that I may (or may not) have indulged in, while I escaped, unscathed, with a self-indulgent *"Dekhechho ki kaando."* (See what a thing to do!) punctuated with some appreciative snortling.

I was given to understand that Moyna di was terrified of ghosts and haunted places. She could be found talking animatedly to anyone who would care to listen, narrating enthralling stories about the return of some haunted spirit of our neighbour who had hanged himself several years ago. Apparently, the spirit had returned to our neighbourhood to complete some unfinished business! I remember seeing my grandma, enraptured, listening to her stories in the evenings, which she dished out quite as effortlessly as her *maccher paturi* and *shukto*.

Now, one afternoon, I was bored out of my wits. Everyone was indulging in their afternoon siesta, while I loitered around aimlessly. A mischievous idea struck me like a bolt from the blue (red, actually.) My father (a doctor) was in charge of vaccinating children that year and had a whole lot of syringes stocked in his cabinet. I had nicked out one or two of them and had hidden them in my room. My grandma used to wear *altaa* on her feet sometimes (a red liquid used to adorn palms/feet). The bottle of *altaa* was kept in her room on the top shelf.

That afternoon, I sneaked into my grandma's room and took the bottle of *altaa*. Then I went into the kitchen and got hold of the potatoes that had been kept aside to be cooked later by Moyna di (some enticing *aloo-bhaajas* were in order for dinner, apparently). I deftly injected each one of the potatoes with some *altaa* with the help of the syringes!

Later in the evening, Moyna di sat leisurely with the *boti* (a cutting instrument, used in all Bengali households) to slice the potatoes. To her horror, a bright red blood-like liquid oozed out from the first potato! She shrieked out in horror and nearly jumped out of her skin! Amidst the hullabaloo that ensued, my mother, aunt and grandma all rushed into the kitchen and tried to ascertain the facts. I stood quietly near the door, observing the scene with subdued nonchalance.

"Bhoo... bhoo... Bhoot" was all that Moyna di managed to gasp, breathlessly, while my mother pacified her by saying that the potato was probably rotten and she should not panic! After much coaxing, Moyna di seemed mollified. She looked askance at the other potatoes but picked up one more with trembling fingers. As she sliced it with the *boti,* a spurt of red liquid splashed all over her saree! (I must have been ultra-generous with the *altaa* on that one.)

There was no restraining her! *"O ma go, ei baari te bhoot ache, amake baanchao."* (Oh my God, there's a ghost in this house, save me!) She shrieked on the top of her lungs and sprinted away from the kitchen, running helter-skelter like a madwoman, with her arms flailing wildly over her head. The ruckus alerted our neighbours (the adventure-seeking types), who rushed over to the scene of the crime and gathered excitedly at the centre of the cacophony.

I stood sheepishly at the corner, wondering whether this time I had gone too far! The whole house was abuzz with curiosity over the blood-spurting tubers! From Maa Kaali's wrath to the afore-mentioned spirit of our hanged neighbour, there were theories galore! Some of our neighbours' calculative speculation would have put Sherlock Holmes to shame!

My mother cornered me that night and I confessed that I was the mastermind behind the premeditated *altaa*-infused vegetables! She went berserk, partly because of Moyna di's plight but mainly (as far as I could tell) because of the unfortunate turn of events that would lead Moyna di to quit and force her to take part in the culinary activities! She threatened me with the quintessential weapon that all Bengali moms have, *"Daara, baba ashuk, baba k bolbo."* (Wait till I tell your dad). Even my most remorseful look, with my tearful, angelic eyes, failed to pacify her!

Thankfully, that evening my Maths test results came out and I had aced the exam (I had got either 49 out of 50 or 50 out 49.) and when my mother told my father about the bloody-potato fiasco, he only chuckled indulgently and then, catching my mother's eye, quickly chided me half-heartedly with a *"toke nie ar para jayna."* (We can't deal with you anymore). My mother gave him a thunderous look and stomped out of the room.

I later learnt that Moyna di had to be cajoled and pampered (bribed) with a few new sarees, some *mishti-paans*, a big box of sweets and some chanachur before she reluctantly returned to cook for us.

Thus, all is well that ends well. We ended up relishing Moyna di's mouth-watering delicacies for several years to come. A little birdie later told me that she even narrates the Mystery of the Bleeding Potatoes to whoever is willing to listen, and this version of the story is now laced with bloodied footprints, whispering voices and an invisible child's spine-chilling screams as well!

The Viva

This happened when I was in the third year of Medical College. Having miraculously survived the first 2 years and passing in subjects like Anatomy, my confidence had soared to dizzying heights! You see, when you have classmates who study 17 hours a day and mumble Biochemistry formulae in their sleep at night (As I found out while staying in the Girls' hostel, much to my chagrin), you wonder whether you have landed in an alien land, since I was never the geeky type. So, we were finally in 3rd year, and from books (colossal textbooks that could be used as a dinner table), we had progressed to seeing actual human patients. The semester exams were more than 2 months away, and we did not have a care in the world.

My best friend Ritu was having a quarter-life crisis, of sorts, and told me that she was in love with a senior (who was seeing someone else). I was spending the night in her room, trying my level best to explain it to her that what she was experiencing was merely a surge of hormones (namely, norepinephrine and dopamine, more popularly known as a 'crush') and would dissipate, into thin air, within 4 months (the shelf-life of the said hormones was not too long, thank heavens!)

However, she was of the unshakeable belief that the lanky, heavily myopic, greasy-haired dude was her soulmate-cum-'true love' (there is treatment available for 'delusion', of course, but it seemed an inopportune moment to mention it to her, owing to the fact that she was sobbing into her pillow then). My elaborate but accurate explanation about 'true love' and the allied subjects (replete with flow-charts and graphs) fell on deaf ears (hers, I mean)! After much philosophical deliberation, debate and psycho-analysis, we fell asleep in the wee hours of the morning.

We were unceremoniously awakened the next morning by the shrill ring of my phone, and were informed, to our utter shock, that we had a surprise viva test within a few hours! Now, I was not the most ardent fan of these bally surprise exams, as I had survived, so far, by cramming the whole syllabus the night before the exam! I sprinted downstairs and glanced at the notice board to see who would be my examiner, and to my utter horror, discovered that it was none other than the infamous Hichki Dey!

Those of my readers who have never had the misfortune of coming within shooting range of this fellow would never understand the terror he had instilled in us! The name of this menacing creature was Dr H.K. Dey, and our seniors (true visionaries) had aptly re-christened him as Hichki Dey, owing to his terrorising and hiccup-inducing quality amongst students! He was notorious for failing students at the drop of a hat in most of the viva exams, and his ruthless grilling had even reduced our class-topper to tears one day in front of our eyes! He could easily scare away the living daylights amongst the most well-prepared lot, and legend had it that he had attributed PTSD amongst many of our seniors even decades later!

I started trembling the moment I saw his name written in BOLD just half an inch away from mine. Cursing myself for not praying enough, I mentally prepared to pack my bags in the evening. Some lines of poetry came to my mind then: "There is no reason why; there is but to do or die." (Great words by Tagore or Shakespeare or some other gentleman, I think, can't remember.)

My viva started exactly at 12 noon, and Hichki sir slithered in, like a cobra. He asked me to examine a 14-year-old girl (patient) and note down the findings. He told me that he would be back in 15 minutes and slithered away into oblivion, for a while.

Looking at my ashen face, the patient (a spunky girl named Pompa) asked me merrily, *"Didi, tomar porikkha?* (You have an exam?)"

I nodded and asked her why she was admitted.

She said, airily, "Oh, I have a stone in my gall-bladder but sir will not ask you that."

Flabbergasted, I asked her how she knew that, and she informed me that Hichki had already taken a viva of some senior that morning! I stared at her incredulously as she rattled off a few life-saving pointers; it would not be too off the mark to state here that I turned to her like a sunflower turns to the sun.

Soon enough, Hichki returned to the ward. I can recall vividly that he looked menacing, like a rhinoceros (a carnivorous rhinoceros would be the 'mot juste' if ever there was one). He looked askance at me and asked me about the findings in the patient.

I rambled incoherently, for a while, about gall-bladder stones, but was cut short by his scheming question: "Why is it not cirrhosis?"

Now, such a question would leave any unarmed student reeling, but Pompa (my informer) had already told me that this was the question that had spelt doom for the senior! Acquainted with the vital information from Pompa, I replied with subtle nonchalance, "Well, sir, cirrhosis mainly affects alcoholics, and this is a young girl. Moreover, she has no fluid retention in her abdomen."

Hichki looked at me suspiciously with his typical 'dung-under-the-nose' expression, and my heart skipped a beat.

My eyes scanned the environment for Paanchu da (the ward-boy) to come and save my life.

Okay, I can understand that you are all flummoxed at this critical juncture in my story, so allow me to digress a little and go back in time.

You see, in the pre-Pompa era, when I had realised the life-threatening predicament that I was facing, I had an escape plan ready. (Surely you did not think I would go on this suicide-mission without a plan. What with my scheming intellect!)

I had gone to Paanchu-da, the ward-boy, with a box full of *nolen-gurer sandesh* (his favourite) and discussed my master plan with him. After 10 minutes into my viva, he was to sneak in and inform Hichki Dey that the seminar (scheduled for that evening) had been preponed and was about to begin in 10 minutes.

Now, anyone who knew Dr Hichki Dey knew that he had one major weakness: food! Those who had seen him, up to his elbows in mutton biryani, in our annual college fest, would even bet their life on the fact! I had never seen him miss a seminar (which was followed by food, of course), and more often than not, he was the first one spotted, piling kilos of chicken kebabs on his plate before we could even venture within one mile of the buffet! He would always sit alone and munch the entrée, sometimes closing his eyes, obviously drifting off into a deep reverie, only punctuated by the audible crunching of bones (chicken, presumably). Polishing off 12 rasgullas at one go was no mean feat, but legend had it that several seniors had seen him do it, without even coming up for fresh air!

Thus, I had bribed Paanchu da with the sandesh, to 'lead him into temptation' and lie to him (not lie, really. Come on, we just tweaked the truth a little bit) and tell him that the seminar was preponed (it was scheduled in the evening, of course).

Soon enough, Paanchu da came in surreptitiously and stuttered, *"Syaar, cinema ta shuru hoe jabe, ei ekhuni hobe"* (The cinema will start.)

Hichki raised one of his massive caterpillar-like eyebrows at him while I looked daggers at Paanchu-da. He obviously had not paid close attention when I was dissecting the finer details of my master plan.

"Cinema?" He asked gruffly.

I coughed politely and budged in at the right cue.

"Cinema? *Maney seminar bolte chao toh?"* (You mean seminar, right?) I asked him, pointedly, giving him a once-in-a-lifetime opportunity to cover up his faux pas.

Paanchu da stuttered, once again, *"Hyaa, hyaa, oi siminaar ta chalu hoe gelo bole, eyi dekhe elum."* (The seminar has just started). Then, after a pregnant pause, he added, for effect, I think, *"Maa kaali bolchi."* (I swear on Maa Kaali).

I glared at Paanchu-da; he was totally overdoing it. Swearing on Goddesses was not part of our afore-mentioned pact (I wanted to shout at him, but did not. Come on, his name was 'Paanchu', for God's sake — he obviously had real 'troubles' in life, unlike you and me.)

I closed my eyes and prayed to all the Gods I knew and slowly opened them to find that my plan had the desired effect. Hichki's face had softened considerably, the ominous clouds had gone, and his eyes shone like stars (no doubt in anticipation of the delicacies that he was fantasising about).

He looked at me and asked, visibly distracted, "Well, where were we?"

"Sir, I had just arrived at the provisional diagnosis after ruling out why cirrhosis seemed an unlikely ailment in the given patient and was enumerating the signs and symptoms of choledocholithiasis, the most likely diagnosis." I rattled off with the smoothness of expensive conditioner (my newfound confidence drawing admiring glances from all the patients nearby, while Pompa stifled a guffaw).

Hichki sir cut me short, glancing at his watch. "Okay, okay, it's getting late. Off you go, then."

He seemed to have about as much interest in my viva as a vegetarian had for Chicken tikka!

He shimmied away and disappeared into the horizon while I fled the scene, holding onto my dear life.

I remember doing a victory dance the moment I entered the hostel and narrating my story of triumph to an enraptured audience! It goes without saying that, after the success of my master plan and some timely help of the fairy Godmother (disguised as Pompa, of course), passing that viva was a no-brainer!

Thus, all is well that ends well. Pompa became my friend; I used to visit her whenever I got time and gifted her (on her request) a set of glass bangles, the day she got discharged. Shockingly, my friend Ritu ended up marrying that greasy-haired senior after a few years (making me realise, with a jolt, that I too can be wrong at times!) Her love story reminded me of the 'Gift of the Magi' (there was no gift, of course, and certainly no 'magi'. Sorry, I have no idea why I drew that comparison). Dr Hichki was captured on her wedding video, taking fourth helpings of dessert from her rather elaborate wedding feast.

Oh, how I miss those days.

My Big Fat Wedding

This is the story of my wedding – written on popular demand… well, not popular… just one person asked me to write it. But still, I felt it was my duty! It was a hotchpotch, topsy-turvy tale that came into being because of my decision to marry a Marwari (Jain) boy!

Allow me to start from the morning of the wedding.

Actually, the chaos had started much earlier. When I disclosed the idea of getting married to my father, his first question was, *"Chhele ta ki? Bangaal na Ghoti?"* (Does the groom have a Bangladeshi origin, or is he originally from West Bengal?)

The Bengali readers will understand why the question seemed so obvious, while good luck to the others if they understand that!

His question hit me like a ton of bricks! It was like after preparing for the History exam, you are slapped with the Physics question paper instead. I had no answer, and I fled the scene. My sister had to break the ghastly news to him, the day after.

There was the usual cacophony, warnings about the intercultural clash, and the same old drama and coaxing (from my side) about our undying love and whatnot.

Anyway, both the families were cajoled, and after a few meetings, my big fat wedding was chalked out.

Let us not digress. I will start afresh.

Now, my mother had passed away, and I did not rely too much on any of my female relatives but prepared for the said wedding single-handedly (my father, an extremely busy doctor, seemed only too happy to let me undertake this humongous task). I had asked my husband (boyfriend, then) how many guests would come from his side of the family and had mentally prepared for the answer to be 100 or thereabouts. However, he told me at least 600 guests would come from his side (add 300 from my side), bringing the total to a staggering 900! After doing this quick mental Math, my eyebrows were raised so high that they had a risk of permanently disappearing into my hairline! However, I did not let my anxiety show and practised some deep breathing and yoga techniques to calm myself and told myself... "Yes, you can do it."

After doing the preliminary work (i.e. deciding the venue, hiring the caterer, bribing the priest to wrap up the wedding mantras in 15-20 minutes, etc), we were all set!

I had arranged for the wedding '*tattvas*' (gifts) to be gift-wrapped suitably (me and my cousins wrapped several gifts overnight and till date are the fastest gift-wrappers in this side of the country) and the veg and non-veg food to be served on different floors so that the vegetarians would not get a whiff of the non-veg food being served. (Here the word 'whiff' has been used literally as well as figuratively).

The wedding trousseau was bought, the invitation-cards distributed, the cameraman/videographer hired (Thank God, there were no ghastly pre-wedding shoots those days.) and I was all set for the D-day!

It would not be entirely out of order to mention here that I always follow a 'to-do' list and like to be well-prepared for everything. (I even read a book on divorce on the eve of my wedding.)

The evening of the wedding came (slowly and menacingly, like a storm), and the guests had just started flooding in. My jaw was already aching from all the forced smiling in front of the cameras and guests. But I braved the storm and beamed at all and sundry — one beatific smile at a time!

I was told by my grandmother that touching the feet of the elders would earn me several brownie points, so I made a dive for anyone near me. Although there were a few mishaps here and there, such as me touching the feet of the cameraman's crew and some second-cousin who was 7 years younger than me (not my fault, he looked like a decade older than me), all in all, everyone was convinced that I was the perfect demure bride!

Then came the hordes of Marwadi ladies (each one wearing a saree/lehenga which was far more gorgeous than my wedding trousseau and adorned with more jewellery than my whole family put together). They fussed over me, and one lady literally weighed my gold necklace with her hand (her face uncomfortably only half an inch away from mine), but I braved it all like the great Bengali Freedom Fighters!

The groom arrived on a white horse, resplendent in a typical Rajasthani princely ensemble, complete with a feather-in-the-turban and all. However, a stampede of my aunts (Bengali) ensued, jostled him away, and he emerged a few minutes later, unrecognisable in a plain white dhoti and vest, looking bewildered (Bengali wedding attire). The Marwadi clan looked mortified at the disrobing of their prince but grudgingly accepted it after my aunts informed them that it was our custom (after being bribed with hot, savoury snacks, they seemed suitably mollified).

Thereafter, there was the dancing by all the Marwadis (the quintessential *'sangeet'* had started in full vogue and caught my Bong members completely off-guard). I saw most of my family members looking askance at the dancing folks and a few mumbling (a little too loudly, to be polite, *"Jotto shob."* (Too much.)

I had foreseen this predicament, and at my prearranged hand gesture, my sister and cousins quickly came over and ushered my hubby and me (the bride and the groom) to the stage too.

After around 20 minutes of dancing, I found (to my pleasant surprise) that all the Bengali folks were on-stage too (they obviously couldn't stay away from the 'hip' Bollywood song-list that I had selected, along with a few 'in' Bangla-band songs of Bhoomi/Chandrabindu, etc, which were in vogue those days).

Before one could say 'cuckoo', all my aunts were dancing away and the uncles (they all had a drinking binge earlier in someone's room and we all pretended that we didn't know about it) joined in too and started grooving to the beats (as to why they indulged in the Durga Puja *bhaashaan*-moves, I don't have the foggiest idea. It beats me till date and gives me nightmares).

The auspicious time for the wedding rituals was just minutes away (the *'shubho mahurat'*), but they all threw caution to the wind and danced like there was no tomorrow.

They had to be literally dragged offstage, and it was announced grimly that the rituals would start.

The chanting of the mantras did not last long (according to my pact with the priest), and all the while, people kept glancing at their watches. (Waiting to dig in, no doubt, gluttons!) The ceremony, per se, was pretty uneventful (Thank God).

In my haste, I had all but forgotten about the big 'fish *tattva*'! For those of you who are unaware, it is a Bengali wedding tradition that a bride has to be gifted with a big fish (raw, obviously) from the groom's side. The fish symbolises good luck and prosperity, and the gesture of the groom's family gifting the bride is their way of extending their wishes for her happiness as she embarks upon the new journey or whatever.

Now, there was no question about me asking for a raw fish from my husband's Jain family (they would probably cancel the wedding at my audacity)! However, I had to pacify my folks (Bengali) too, because they would feel offended if the fish wasn't offered by the groom's side!

Having a scheming intellect since childhood (or maybe my remarkable IQ thanks to all the fish I consumed), I was well-prepared for this...er... 'fishy' turn of events! I quickly gestured to my sister, who went to the room where all the gifts were kept and returned with a huge, garishly decorated gift tray!

It was a gigantic, gift-wrapped sandesh (fish-shaped), and everyone let out a collective exclamation as I explained that my in-laws had gifted it to me, and, being vegetarians, they could not possibly gift me real fish. They nodded sympathetically and patted my head (probably trying to console me because I was marrying into a vegetarian family), and I heaved a sigh of relief... Phew! The fish predicament was over!

Then, I scurried about a bit, throwing the customary lame questions here and there: "*Apni bhalo kore kheyechen toh?*" (Did you eat properly? Obviously, I saw you stuffing your face and it's there in my wedding-video too. In case you want to watch it, be my guest; if you have masochistic desires, that is.) and answering to equally lame questions: "*Oma, tui koto boro hoye gechis!*" (You have grown up so much! Er, it's not like I had a choice. Did I?) and "*Accha, Bengali-log ullulululu kyun karte hain?*" (Er, why don't you go away forever to Honolulu instead of asking me these stupid questions?) I smiled serenely and nodded along and kept answering these million-dollar questions, one at a time!

After what seemed like years, the wedding was finally over, and I was so relieved! However, my relief was short-lived as I noticed a few anxious faces amongst the throng and a few of my aunts tut-tutting and craning their necks to look at me disapprovingly! My heart skipped a beat, something was definitely amiss!

I quickly went to the loo and checked my reflection. Well, I looked okay (As goofy and awkward as any blingy-saree clad bride, that is). For the life of me, I could not fathom the reason behind the not-so-subtle disapproving looks.

Then, seeing my quizzical look, my maid informed me that it was time for '*bidaai*' and any self-respecting bride would dissolve in copious amounts of tears now and sob uncontrollably into her father's arms, while, here I was, dry-eyed and stony-faced!

Now, I have to say I didn't see this coming. Forever shy of expressing any emotions (and never having cried in public ever!), I was at a complete loss as to what to do! I thought of the movie *Titanic* (the scenes where I had cried) and the tear-jerker novels too, but, the tears (Like a flighty mistress) just did not come in my time of need! I was running out of time, and the anxiety of not being able to cry turned me into a bundle of nerves! Then, a eureka-like idea struck me — I gave a loud gasp and, hiding my face with both hands, escaped into the loo.

I quickly opened my purse and took out my contact-lens solution (never thought I'd thank God for my myopia, one day) and squeezed the bottle liberally into both my eyes. I emerged, triumphantly, a moment later, with tears streaming down my cheeks and my eyes suitably red and watery. I would have gotten all the trophies for being the perfect damsel in distress (or bride in unbridled tears or whatever.)

Anyway, I may have overdone it a bit (I had dabbled in theatre in my school-days, you see.) because some of my aunts were actually concerned at my semi-convulsions and thought a bout of hysteria had come upon me or a panic-attack! Afterwards, I dabbed my eyes with a huge handkerchief someone had handed me and sniffed too loudly (for a lady, definitely) and all was well!

The agony of the wedding was finally over (and the agony of marriage had just begun), but let's call it a 'happy ending', for now.

Today, I chanced upon a young girl complaining in Facebook that she cannot have a big fat Indian wedding (due to the pandemic) and I shake my head in disbelief ("Lucky girl, if only I could have gotten away with getting married with 50 guests only") Anyway, the grass on the other side always looks greener (just like my diet post-marriage, which looks considerably greener).

Sole-Mates

Okay, so I received an email asking me to write a piece for this ultra-girly blog, and I was initially psyched. However, I was bummed out when they told me the topic: 'Soulmates'!

So, here goes nothing.

(Spoiler alert: This piece is not for the die-hard romantics. It is my take on soulmates, viz., "Do they really exist?")

Since time immemorial, we have been fed with the concept of soulmates by movies/rom-coms, novels, magazines, friends, etc. You are supposed to wander lonely through life (or is it the woods?) and then bump into someone who is, apparently, your 'soulmate'. Then, all the unanswered questions in your life are answered, and you are supposed to hear violins playing in the background, and the days seem sunnier and so on and so forth. It will mark the end of your life as you know it and thus, will begin the second phase of your life. Your life is suddenly a series of lazy, long summer afternoons (yes, even if you have a job) with special emphasis on waterfalls and roses lurking somewhere in the background. Also, for some reason, dusk is the high-point of your day, peppered with all sorts of pinkish hues and rain (and quite possibly rainbows if I'm not mistaken) and so on and so forth. You get the picture, right? All the mundane stuff will disappear from your life faster than you can say cuckoo, and you will spend long hours gazing at the stars (or maybe into each other's eyes), and all the romantic songs will suddenly have meaning.

If you have been fed with romanticism long enough, you will grow up believing in all this.

This concept is perfect in every sense, except that it is supposed to work for humans who are generous, loving, pure, and kindred spirits, looking for other generous, loving, pure, and kindred spirits. However, in my experience, most of us (including yours truly) are not generous, loving, pure, kindred spirits but are damaged folks with anxiety issues on the verge of insanity (with the emotional range of a teaspoon). So, this disturbing concept of two disturbed people uniting and creating some kind of magic sounds disturbing.

It brings us to point no. 2 (or 3, I'm not sure), viz., 'be yourself'. It is often said that in front of your soulmate, you can 'be yourself', i.e., show your true colours without being judged or poisoned. They will love you for who you are. Yes, they will love you with all your flaws, smile indulgently at your short temper, roll in laughter at your lame repetitive jokes and still find you attractive — even in a monkey cap!

However, I find this concept quite disturbing, once again. I think that to act and behave like our true selves is the kind of third-degree torture, and you should not force it on anyone (especially someone you claim to love). Imagine the agony of living with the full dimensions of someone equally crazy like you, and to entertain their temper tantrums and not roll your eyes, ever so often, at them. Yes, in the early stages of 'love' when you share your secrets and your deepest fears with someone and they empathise with you, then you do feel very liberated.

Add to that, the mix of the hormones (high levels of dopamine and norepinephrine) that are released in the initial stages of attraction, which causes the giddying, energetic 'high' — the euphoria, insomnia, stammering and sweaty palms (you make an absolute fool of yourself). All of these are NOT the same inner awakenings due to the soulmate thingy, but are emotions driven by hormones, controlled by the reward centre of your brain (the ventral tegmental area and caudate nucleus). It has been scientifically proven that this region of our brain gets activated like crazy when you fall 'in love' (this feeling of attraction is extremely addictive because the same brain region is affected when you get a high from cocaine – not that I'm saying that you use cocaine as an alternative to soulmates, no sir).

However, when you are in love/attracted to someone, this temporary 'high' from the hormones shuts off another very important area in our brain that regulates critical thinking and rational behaviour (in short, love/attraction makes you dumb). Have you ever done something embarrassingly stupid, when in love, that you wouldn't otherwise? No? Perhaps I should ask a young Shakespearean couple to get the correct answer.

So, 'love' as we know it, can be the thing that makes you want to do ghastly stuff like rush out of bed early in the morning or the thing that makes you want to never leave your bed the whole day. And a person who elicits such irrational behaviour from us can never be good for our souls, right?

Also, another equally silly concept I have heard is that your soulmates are supposed to understand you without you having to say a word, right? C'mon, please.

This magical, intuitive understanding, i.e. 'understanding without saying a word,' can be charming on paper but not so much in real life when your 'soulmate' is sulking the whole day because you did not understand their feelings and have hurt them by saying something that they won't say because you are supposed to understand them without they saying it. Sounds like gibberish, right? That's probably because it is!

Our hobbies range from reading to travelling to cooking, but we are not professional 'mind readers', are we? (And is there such a profession, by any chance?) Bollocks, I say! In fact, it would be better if we articulated our thoughts clearly, using paragraphs and correct punctuation, and enunciated (please, guys, I hate folks who mumble). The world would be a better place if you were properly informed of the actual scientific reasons and statistical analysis of complex actions such as sulking, grumbling, and suddenly becoming as silent as the 'g' in lasagna.

The last point I want to make is that the concept of soulmates assumes that a particular person will ensure you are always happy and never lonely. This concept sounds even more absurd than any song of Baadshah! We must understand that we alone are entirely responsible for our own happiness. If you put the entire responsibility of your happiness on someone else's shoulders, not only are you burdening them with unrealistic and inhuman expectations, but you are signing up for a lifetime of misery by raising the bar so high that no man or animal can ever climb it. Let us not put any human on a pedestal (like God) and write off any chance of happiness we may have had with the poor creature, if we see them just as they are, viz., flawed and not very useful. Also, it is difficult when you are forced to do things that you are not qualified to do (like being nice to dumb folks).

Look, all of us have all the bearings of having grown up, but we are still, in fact, a small child! We are needy, we constantly need validation, we are constantly hungry (Sorry, that's irrelevant), we do not like to be reprimanded for our shortcomings, and we constantly crib! Moreover, we have the added responsibility of behaving like adults all the time (because, for some strange reason, most adults prefer other adults to behave like adults!)

We must realise that the person we love is neither perfect nor our twin souls; they are just, in fact, an idiot (like ourselves). Yes, they are a lovable idiot who is bound to goof-up sometimes and be Miss Snarky or Mr Whiny on certain days (most of the days). Sometimes, they are just plain lazy (there is no excuse for laziness, but if you have one, please let me know). On some days, you will just want to shout out certain words at them that will make the Pope cry, and on better days, they appear to be like a plateful of veggies — you eat them because you have to, not because you want to, much like accepting the bland truths in life (ugh!).

This is why you need a sense of humour to realise that your imperfect mate is goofy in most of the ways, but is still lovable and deserves accolades for tolerating you this long and for not saying aloud the mean, horrible and accurate things that they think about you. In short, both of you are like the soles of a pair of shoes (both the soles need to function for a person to walk in life, viz, sole-mates!). So, if folks tell you that finding your soulmate is like a spiritual thing, please ask them to be more specific (demons are spirits too, you know).

Moral of the Story: There is no sunshine or waterfalls all the time. In fact, there is not a single waterfall in my city. This obsession with water bodies (waterfalls, rain, rivers, and estuaries), rainbows, flowers, dusk and soulmates has got to STOP!